S0-ABA-095

Also by Clarissa Watson
Published by Ballantine Books:

THE BISHOP IN THE BACK SEAT

RUNAWAY

Clarissa Watson

BALLANTINE BOOKS • NEW YORK

Library of Congress Catalog Card Number: 84-45633

ISBN 0-345-33114-1

This edition published by arrangement with Atheneum

Manufactured in the United States of America

First Ballantine Books Edition: June 1986

For my husband

One

The sun was as pale and wan as I was. It was not quite eight A.M., an hour in late March when neither human nor heavenly bodies in Gull Harbor are quite prepared to face another day.

My aunt, Lydia Wentworth, was an exception. But then, she was always an exception. And right now she was cantering along in front of me with the revolting *joie de vivre* of a drill sergeant leading his luckless charges off to a harrowing day in the field.

There she was, in her dove gray riding habit, her right leg hooked elegantly around the saddle pommel, sitting as easily as if she were serving afternoon tea. Well, she'd been brought up with her right leg hooked around a side-saddle pommel. As had I, thanks to her. Only today I was riding astride and in jeans—you don't ride side-saddle on an out-of-control locomotive.

She'd been turning up at my house like this for two weeks. Never any advance warning—she'd just suddenly appear, clattering around in my driveway, riding her favorite gray mare, towing some bad actor for me, and halooing and whistling until she roused me from my downy cot and sweet dreams. I do not approve of violent activity in the early morning, and to me eight A.M. is dawn. Sleep is the only civilized pastime at that hour.

She kept a fair sized stable at her estate, The Crossing. Mostly the horses were retirees from her rather extensive

1

racing establishment and the majority had mouths of iron and manners to match, as I was finding out.

"What you need is some challenging exercise," Aunt Lydie had announced to me in her most formidable voice when I came back from France after a disastrous affair. "You're drooping about. Why is it that you are always attracted to scoundrels? Why can't you fall in love with that nice Oliver Reynolds? Oh, well . . . so am I, I suppose. And I can tell you that there are only two cures for a broken heart . . . violent exercise or a new lover."

She had been subjecting me to the first ever since and it was getting exhausting. I was afraid the morning canters would go on with increasing vigor until either I found a new man or she ran out of spirited horses. It was all very well for her to go careening along ahead of me on her gray mare—the mare, after all, was a model of perfect gaits and manners. Whereas I was being subjected to nothing less than the rack.

There had been rain sometime during the night so that the occasional fugitive drop slipping from a branch made a surprisingly loud noise as it fell, even above the muffled sound of our passing. From the corner of my eye I was aware of spears of onion grass rising from the brown forest cover and the rust of mosses greening themselves for spring.

La Coquette, my aunt's mare, bobbed along like a goody-goody little girl on her way to dancing class. My snorting steed and I plunged along in her delicate wake like a bark in a killing sea, with me standing up in my stirrups and almost falling on my horse's neck in an effort to keep from running my aunt and her mount straight into the ground. My arms had turned to spaghetti: a hundred and eight pounds of thirty-six-and-a-half-year-old female are no match for a ten ton Goliath.

We rocketed along like this for another ten minutes or so. I was puffing and out of breath. Godzilla (as I had mentally christened him) was, on the other hand, just get-

2

ting into the spirit of things, if his death grip on the bit was any indication. I prayed for succor. An earthquake. A cyclone. A hurricane. Any act of God that would end the torment. I am too old to be fighting with a horse.

What I got was a flock of geese.

They were a tightly disciplined flock of Canadas and they came sweeping in very low, a winged fighter squadron hedge-hopping across the countryside. The noise was deafening, a mad cacophony of quacks and honks and automobile horn noises.

Godzilla decided instantly that he had been strafed. He took off as if he had a ticking bomb underneath his tail, almost knocking my aunt and her mare off their feet.

"Give him his head," Aunt Lydie screamed thinly after my fast disappearing form. "Give him his head and he'll go home!"

Give him his head? He already had it. And the bit. And anything else his heart desired.

We burst out of the woods like a rocket and took to the open fields, acres of which—carefully fenced—surround every noteworthy property in Gull Harbor . . . and there are plenty of them. I had absolutely not the foggiest idea of where we were . . . first of all I was too busy trying to cling to the mad monstrosity beneath me to chart a course and secondly I was accustomed to approaching people's houses by the front drive like a lady and not from the surrounding fields, like the Mau Mau. Ordinarily I can ride a horse with a piece of very thin thread in its mouth; but this was ridiculous—my arms were coming out at the sockets. If it was an athletic contest (and it was), I was already a loser.

I glanced over my shoulder just once and saw my aunt lift her mare's head, turn her neatly, and gallop off in the direction from which we'd come. Probably gone to get an ambulance and reserve a bed in the Gull Harbor hospital, I thought bitterly as she vanished.

After that I kept my full attention on the business of

3

staying aboard, with visions of broken bones and full body casts to help keep me focused on the importance of staying exactly where I was, however uncomfortable it might seem at the moment.

As far as my boggled eye could see there were fields and post-and-rail fences and more fields and brush hedges and so on, apparently ad infinitum. Godzilla saw the same thing and liked what he saw—he was snorting with excitement, exactly like a dragon, only there weren't any flames. He was on course and galloping like an express train—head up, ears switching back and forth, assessing the landscape. I had this weird feeling that I was in the hands of a professional.

We skimmed through the first jump, making the hedge rock. Before I even caught my breath we were approaching a second well-pruned hedge. Godzilla took it so deep into the branches that I felt them graze my hips. I could just imagine my aunt Lydie sitting on a hilltop, surveying the slightly disorganized scene, and saying with unabashed self-satisfaction, "You see, Persis, what a little exercise will do for you?"

The next few fences were post and rail and Godzilla treated them with respect, clearing them cleanly and neatly. He was beginning to get the feel of the course.

Now there were more hedges. Godzilla stood off and took them from a great distance, plunging deep into them to save time and energy. I wondered if my legs were bleeding beneath my jeans.

Godzilla was pacing himself now. He wasn't even puffing. I began to relax and enjoy the ride just the littlest bit. The crazy old beggar seemed to know exactly what he was doing, which was certainly more than I could say of myself.

Rather to my surprise, I recognized one of the houses that flashed by in the distance as we pursued our hurly-burly course across the meadows . . . I'd been on that particular terrace many times for cocktails. I was an accepted

4

fixture at all the social events in Gull Harbor. Not because I was Persis Willum, starving artist . . . Gull Harborites are not impressed by starvation. On the contrary, I was welcome because I was the niece (albeit an impoverished one) of Lydia Wentworth, who just happened to be one of the wealthiest women in the world. Furthermore, I was youngish, not bad looking, and knew which fork to use at table. Put it all together and you have all the ingredients you need for social success in Gull Harbor. Not that it mattered to me.

This particular terrace belonged to Elmsworth, one of the great mansions of the North Shore. And that meant we were on our way to The Crossing—admittedly by a circuitous route but nonetheless on our way. My foxy old traveling companion of the moment knew exactly where he was and what he was doing. Next would come Blairfield, carted over rock by rock and stone by stone from Italy in 1889 by old Ramsey Blair. Then we would be at Tribute, Courtney Lassiter's modest but elegant holding that was the last bastion before the nine hundred acres of Lydia Wentworth's The Crossing, the greatest property of them all. I decided by some quick calculation that we would have traveled approximately four miles . . . the exact distance of the Maryland Hunt Cup, which I had been told the equine monster beneath me had won twice when he was in his salad days.

Visions of our arrival at the stables now overwhelmed me, the scarcely concealed sniggers of the grooms already ringing in my ears. The horse would be lathered up and foam covered . . . an unpardonable sin. I would be wind-whipped, perspiring, and disheveled . . . equally unpardonable sins. They would whisper behind my back as they cooled Godzilla out. It wasn't fair, I told myself resentfully.

We charged across Blairfield's horizon. And, I thought, still dwelling on my impending arrival at The Crossing, I shall have to beg for a ride home. Too awful.

Blairfield disappeared astern and the high hedges of Tribute rose up in the distance. The moment I saw them, all concern for my arrival at Aunt Lydie's disappeared. If Godzilla attempted those hedges I might never arrive at Aunt Lydie's at all.

Tribute was an exception to the general North Shore landscape. A neat, four acre, hedge-enclosed square, it was plunked down between the two giant estates of Blairfield and The Crossing as if a monster pinking scissors had made a slight mistake in cutting out their mutual border. A long, narrow driveway, like a breathing tube, ran down to it from the tree-lined road that marked the southern edge of the estates, and Tribute itself was completely invisible from the road. It was a surprising little place—unexpected in that particular setting. The present English owner had made it more surprising by enclosing it in high hedges.

And I knew those hedges: they were killers. Five feet tall and a good three feet in width. Worst of all, they concealed a chain link fence topped with barbed wire. A member of the Gull Harbor police force had told me about it. "A regular fortress," he'd said, approvingly. The local police thought we should all arm ourselves to the teeth and take extraordinary precautions in these days of increasing robberies.

I saw those hedges looming up at me, ever bigger, and I began to pull desperately on the left rein, hoping to turn the horse so that he would make a slight detour and thus miss Tribute completely. Godzilla had seen the hedges—his ears were pointed straight at them—and it appeared he had no intention of avoiding their challenge. I pulled with all my strength. His neck did not bend. He took dead aim and we charged, devouring the intervening field in a ground-eating gallop. A great mushroom cloud of impending doom seemed to rise and hover over us.

The hedges came nearer and nearer. I wondered if it was too late in my ill-spent life to pray. Visions of smashed

6

and broken equine and human backs and necks and legs flashed in front of my eyes.

Godzilla changed his tempo. He seemed to gather himself together, giving his tail an extra flip, like a rocket charge. I felt him shudder. I closed my eyes. And we were flying through the air, branches smashing around us. There was plenty of sudden, crackling noise with our passage.

Then we hit the ground, right lead foot first and the rest following smoothly—he didn't even stumble. I snatched at the reins, helping him lift his head up for balance, and we continued on our way, not pausing to consider the damage behind us. We had landed on deep green lawns behind the one-story miniature French château. My quick glance made note of imposing copper beeches surrounded by ivy, cement urns filled with more ivy, friendly sculptures in stone of squirrels and a fox, brick pathways winding here and there, and the kind of furniture one leaves outside year round.

This outdoor furniture had been set up, as if for a meeting, at the far side of the garden. And until the moment of our entry, it had been occupied by about a half dozen men who appeared to have been concentrating their attention on a collection of papers spread out on a glass-topped metal table. With our explosive appearance on the scene, they scattered as if they had been bombed, quite as astonished to see Godzilla and me as we were to be there.

I had no time to dwell on the intricacies of the situation: my horse was crossing the lawn in great spine-jolting leaps, sinking deep into the well-kept turf with every step, and the hedge at the far side of the property was coming at us all too fast. That he had cleared the first seemed miraculous. Could he do it again?

I was dimly aware of a cacophony of shouts and what sounded like curses from the garden behind me but there was no time for apologies. I leaned far forward in the saddle to take my weight off the horse's back and help make the impossible jump possible. Godzilla punched his way in

7

and out of the spongy lawn—a kangaroo on a pogo stick. He gathered himself together and hurled his body at the greenery as if at an adversary. We were airborne, soaring. It was lovely. Something whizzed by on my left. I paid no attention. Probably throwing rocks at me, I thought. Never mind, I'll apologize tomorrow. Meanwhile, we're flying. We're over. I'm safe.

Godzilla alighted on the other side of Tribute's enclosure with a certain air of self-congratulation, well pleased to see that he had not lost his touch. We were on Wentworth land now, and he seemed to know it. He began to ease himself up—although he was by no means winded by his efforts—falling from a gallop to a slow canter to an easy, swinging trot. I was overjoyed to realize that we would not, after all, appear at The Crossing's stables lathered and foaming. Horse and rider would arrive together at the barn in more or less decorous partnership. I would make up something to explain Aunt Lydie's absence.

And tomorrow morning—or even better, this very afternoon—I would hie myself over to Sir Courtney Lassiter's house, bearing armloads of flowers, to apologize for wrecking his beautiful lawn, already green so early in the spring.

Within ten minutes we were clattering into the cobble-stoned Tudor stableyard, more or less cooled out and in reasonably good order, I thought.

The first groom to see us, who happened also to be the head groom, shattered my illusions.

"Mrs. Willum," he cried. "Whatever happened to you?"

I couldn't believe it. How could he possibly know what I had been through? How could he possibly have read the ignominy of my morning's adventure?

"What-do-you-mean-whatever-happened?" I mumbled, swinging myself down from the by now docile steeplechaser. That's when the pain hit me for the first time . . . when I braced myself with my left hand to vault out of the

8

saddle. It wasn't exactly pain, really . . . the sensation was more that of a sharp and relentless stinging.

I looked at my arm, where the head groom was also staring, horrified. The sleeve of my Brooks Brothers cotton shirt was nicked and a torrent of bright red, healthy looking blood had issued from the neat little aperture.

I unbuttoned my cuff and pulled up the sleeve to expose my upper arm. No question about it, the blood was mine— my very own. The groom and I looked at each other.

"A branch?" I asked. "We were jumping. . . ."

He shook his head and gave rapid orders to an underling who was standing next to us, holding Godzilla's head. There was something about bandages . . . there are always plenty of bandages in a stable, even though they're generally used for wrapping horses' legs.

Then he turned back to me.

"A branch," I repeated. But I saw doubt and curiosity in his eyes.

I stared down at my arm.

Then I remembered. There had been *something* when we took the last hedge—something whizzing by.

But it was absurd. Courtney Lassiter mistake me for an intruder? He would have recognized me at once. Courtney Lassiter shoot at a woman? Never. He was a gentleman.

No—it was absolutely out of the question. People in Gull Harbor shoot at clay pigeons, live pigeons, assorted unfortunate wild game, occasional rabbits and crows (although these latter are rather frowned on), but never, absolutely *never* at dogs, foxes, horses, or people riding with or on them. And Courtney Lassiter of all people? Out of the question.

I looked the head groom firmly in the eye. "A branch," I repeated with finality. Then I marched up to the big house to wait for Aunt Lydie to make her appearance and arrange to have me driven home. I would ask if I could stop at Tribute to apologize to whoever was in residence and offer to repair the damage Godzilla and I had done to the lawn.

9

In due time she appeared, every silver-blond silken hair in place, exuding unruffled elegance. I don't think even being run away with would have disturbed her eternal savoir-faire.

I made my suggestion: could we stop at Tribute on the way home? Would the chauffeur (my aunt did not drive) mind? I'd made such a mess of the lawn. . . .

To my astonishment she refused.

"But Aunt Lydie, that mad horse of yours jumped right over Courtney's hedges. I ruined the lawn. I ought at least to. . . ."

"Absolutely not."

"But. . . ."

"Persis, I forbid it."

"But I. . . ."

"Persis, I have the keys to Tribute. Courtney left them with me. He always does."

Then it dawned on me. Courtney Lassiter had not been present among the men in his own backyard. Of course . . . there had been a note in the gossip column of the *Gull Harbor Trumpet* yesterday afternoon and I'd forgotten it until now. "About that devastating Courtney Lassiter," it said. "Rumor has it he will not return from the south of France for another two weeks or so, a bit of news that will leave the local belles desolate."

So Courtney Lassiter was away on another of what Aunt Lydie referred to as his "marvelously mysterious disappearances." Well, there was nothing new about that—he came and went from the Gull Harbor scene with the independence of a reasonably affluent and active international bachelor of advanced middle age.

But if he was indeed still in France, who was at Tribute? Why a meeting outdoors; as far as possible from the house and its amenities? Why so early in the morning? *Was* it a meeting after all?

I began to understand.

"You mean that the people I told you I saw shouldn't have been . . . ?"

"It is a distinct possibility, Persis."

"Then don't you think we ought to call the police?" I reached for the telephone.

"No. Wait."

I still had my hand on the phone. It was on a Queen Anne table directly beneath a Velázquez. It was the first, and probably the only time in my life, I did not pause to admire the painting.

I stared instead at my aunt. She looked a little pale, I thought, even beneath her exquisite ivory everyday pallor.

"No," she repeated. "Bobby Blessing called early this morning to say that I must surrender the keys to no one unless he says it's all right. I assume that includes the police."

"But. . . ."

"No." She was very firm. When my aunt gives an order there is no question of disobedience. "We will not call the police, Persis. Bobby Blessing is the most intelligent man I know. He is the most important. Also, he is Courtney Lassiter's best friend. I trust him implicitly. The police would ask for the keys and I must honor Bobby's request. We will call Bobby Blessing."

"And he will decide . . . ?"

"Exactly. That is precisely what I mean."

And call Bobby Blessing is what we did. I'm still not sure I understood why, but it is what we did.

Instantly.

In the next few minutes my aunt subjected me to a performance that took me straight back to the nursery. She was the Nanny; I was the obedient child.

First I was commanded to give Bobby Blessing a brief telephone account of the episodes at Tribute. I did so, answering his one or two questions as briskly as possible.

Then I was ordered to leave the room while Aunt Lydie

11

continued to chat with him. I did so, standing rather foolishly in the hallway contemplating a Picasso clown, a Turner seascape, and a Monet garden on the wall opposite me.

After a few minutes my aunt put her head out of the library door and commanded me to go downstairs where Roberts, her favorite chauffeur, would be waiting with a car to drive me home.

I protested a little. "But what's going on, anyway? Tell me, please."

The small rebellion was not a success. "Please have the goodness to do as I say, Persis. I'm still on the telephone."

I did as she said. Roberts was waiting, as advertised, and we drove to my house in silence—his polite, mine sulky. I was still sulking as I stripped off my horse-smelling clothes and stepped into the shower, holding my left arm outside the curtain like a fishing pole to keep it dry. This, I sniffed to myself, was *my* adventure, after all. It was Godzilla and I who had stumbled on . . . what had we stumbled on?

Anyway, I had earned by pain and humiliation and a possible bullet wound the right to an explanation of the morning's events. And if no one was willing to give me such an explanation I would be forced to take steps on my own.

Oliver Reynolds, the man I never get around to marrying, has often pointed out that Lydia Wentworth is not the only willful member of the family. And I suppose there is a certain amount of truth to the accusation. In addition to my willful determination not to marry again, he could point out a growing collection of painful scrapes and bruises from other ill-fated and willful adventures, like the disastrous affair with the wrong man in Touquet, France, from which Lydie was helping me to recover, and my chasing missing paintings around the world, which had led to my getting involved with the FBI—and worse.

Except that I wouldn't call such behavior willful: I would

12

say it had more to do with independence, and not liking to be pushed around.

Anyway, I would return to Tribute.

But this time I would not appear as a wild-eyed hoyden on horseback. I would make my second visit as a sedate country lady. With luck, I wouldn't even be recognized.

I pulled my most Gull Harbor, and therefore noncontroversial, sweater and skirt from the closet, placing my confidence in the conservative country Braemar look. A string of not too ostentatious matched pearls—always a symbol of probity. Too bad about the twenty-twenty vision: gold-rimmed eyeglasses would have added a nice touch.

And finally, a Red Cross pin prominently displayed on my bosom.

I surveyed the result in the pier glass mirror. Not too bad an imitation of the golf-bridge-tennis playing matrons of Gull Harbor, I thought. No one would suspect that I was really an artist. Or that I was the recent, unwilling passenger who had crossed the lawn aboard a runaway monster horse. Or, in fact, that I was I.

I noted with special pleasure that there was only the slightest of bulges beneath my yellow sweater to betray the bandage supplied by Lydia Wentworth's head groom and I was further pleased to note that the medication he'd applied with the bandages was doing its stuff . . . all I could feel was a very slight soreness. Aunt Lydie had been saying for years that horse doctors and horse medications were the only ones she would trust, and now I was inclined to agree.

I made one last pass at my unruly hair with the brush and climbed into my Mustang and was off.

The trip back to Tribute was definitely more comfortable than the previous one, although I confess that it didn't seem any faster. Of course, we were now taking the long way around—not half as exciting but infinitely easier on the nervous system. The countryside, in the first tremors of gathering itself to burst into bloom, was calm and peaceful.

13

Seen from the front as I wheeled down the long drive, Tribute looked bland and self-satisfied—the last place on earth where anything especially interesting would be going on. This was deceptive because Tribute had actually been built because of interesting goings-on.

It was an old scandal. Ramsey Blair—the original one—came back from Paris in the nineteen hundreds with a mistress, whom he set up in New York. A. K. Wentworth—Aunt Lydie's grandfather—saw her driving in Central Park and was sorely smitten. The lady liked both gentlemen and refused to choose. Both gentlemen refused to give her up. The result (the men were business tycoons and very pragmatic) was not to duel or to draw straws, but to compromise in the most civilized manner: they built Tribute between their two properties and shared. Eventually the lady acquired enough money and jewels to afford to run away with Blairfield's handsome English butler.

As I approached Tribute, smiling a little at the unconventional arrangement that had caused it to be built, I kept glancing in awe at the hedges that paced my progress, astonished that Godzilla and I had ever succeeded in clearing them safely. They looked bigger and more forbidding than ever from my little car.

The turn-around in front of the house was pure Gull Harbor—adorned by two stone statues (swans, this time), eight big stone urns that would blossom with flowers as the weather warmed, and well-raked bluestone edged neatly with red brick. On either side of the front door were white wrought-iron carriage lamps on standards. Tribute was not a big house—it was more like a graceful pavilion, small and compact. I parked my car, straightened my Red Cross pin, and trotted up to the front door. I pressed the doorbell. Somewhere inside the house musical chimes responded. The door opened with surprising suddenness and I found myself facing a small oriental wearing a cream-colored coat and the subtle but unmistakable politeness of a gentleman's gentleman.

14

"Sssssss?" At least, that's what it sounded like—a word composed solely of S's, like escaping steam.

"Is Mr. Lassiter at home?" I knew he wasn't, but it was a beginning.

"No home, Missy." He began to close the door.

"Just one moment, please." I stuck my foot in the door, giving every indication of being about to enter. "May I speak to whoever is in charge in his absence? It is important."

The oriental gentleman (I had decided, based on nothing at all, that he was Japanese) burst into a long and indignant harangue, from which I extracted the words "all glone," and what sounded like "glood bly." Whatever he was *actually* saying, it was obvious that he was offering me no encouragement, and in an accent that was definitely comic opera.

But I was refusing, as brazenly as I dared, to get the message. "It is a matter of the Red Cross. We are approaching every resident. It is the annual drive. Mr. Lassiter has always been one of our most enthusiastic supporters . . . he will want to see me."

I hoped that some of this speech was penetrating his Eastern composure. Did he understand a word? I couldn't be sure.

Meanwhile we were standing shoulder to shoulder and eye to eye, and looking past his slick black head I could see straight through the drawing room and out the large French doors in back. The outdoor furniture was back in place on the terrace. No one appeared to be around. Most curious of all, I could see no sign of the torn-up earth Godzilla's hoofs had left behind: every single piece of turf had been replaced.

"Missy glo now?" The manservant's glossy black eyes were fixed on mine.

I looked back at him, wondering.

All of us in Gull Harbor leave house keys with our neighbors when we go away . . . in case of broken pipes, burglaries, fire, or any of the hundred and one crises that occur when a house is left empty. Aunt Lydie was Lassiter's nearest neighbor, even though the distance between their houses was measured in acres rather than feet. Since Lassiter often traveled, she probably had her own set of keys.

A manservant would also have a set and he might very well have returned in advance of his master to get the house in order. But I didn't recognize him, although I'd often been a guest at Tribute. Of course it was perfectly possible that he was a new servant. Then who were the people I'd seen on the lawn? Why had they been admitted in Lassiter's absence? Where were they now? What had they been up to? I didn't like this black-eyed sibilant stranger.

And his coat didn't fit.

I tried once more, already feeling defeated. "I should like to speak to Mr. Lassiter if he's in residence. If he's not here, I should like to know where I can reach him and when he will return." I used my most imperious voice, copied faithfully—after years of study—from my aunt's. If this little hissing teakettle was legitimate, he would surely respond to the notes of command.

He responded, all right. But I couldn't understand any of the tirade that followed—most of it was in what I supposed to be Japanese, with a word or two of English tossed in at random. But something in his stance—a sort of over-all tensing of his body—convinced me not only that he had understood everything I'd said but that he was an interloper. An intruder.

He didn't belong here. I was suddenly sure of it. Tribute probably had an elaborate burglar alarm system—everybody in the area does these days. But given know-how and time, even the most elaborate and sophisticated protection system can be circumvented. If this was the typical Gull Harbor installation, it would send an alarm directly to the Gull Harbor police. To neutralize the system? Simple . . . cut the telephone wires.

I backed out of the doorway. He followed, still talking in a high staccato. I edged gingerly toward my car, intent on making a quick departure. I scanned the grounds as far as I could see on both sides of the house in a sort of desperate last look around before climbing into my car. He closed the door behind me, probably happy to see me go.

Then I saw the telephone pole, looking like only a telephone pole in beauty-conscious Gull Harbor could look, namely not like a telephone pole at all but like a part of the breathtaking landscape, or as much so as man could arrange. Only someone as determined as I would have noticed it hiding among the evergreens at an aesthetically pleasing distance from the house and dressed, greenly, in climbing vines.

I was out of the car instantly and across the lawn, poking about among the vines. And there it was—dangling like a participle at the end of an extremely long and embarrassing sentence. A cut wire.

The oriental gentleman's voice came from behind me. "Would you care," he said in faultless English, "to step inside?"

I would not care to. Most definitely. But I had no choice. He struck like a cobra. One of his arms locked around my neck. The other twisted my arm behind my back.

I tried to keep my head—remember what to do. Kick . . . kick backward at his knees. Kick hard and he'll loosen his grip.

But he didn't. So much for what they tell you about self-defense.

I tried to claw at the arm around my neck. It was no contest. I remember thinking—he's so little . . . how can he be so strong? The arm around my neck increased its pressure relentlessly. I couldn't breathe.

I thought, this time I've really done it. This time I'm going to die.

Aunt Lydie and Oliver will be furious.

17

Two

My first thought—purely automatic—was, I don't suppose that I shall ever be able to speak again.

Then my unfocused eyes sorted themselves out and registered the form that was bending over me and I wondered, if I have died and gone to heaven, why did I wait so long?

I was instantly ashamed. There is something déclassé about getting carried away with the first presentable man that comes along. Part of it could have been relief and gratitude: he was holding me in his arms (and not as if he intended to murder me) and gently pouring brandy, drop by drop, down my throat. It was like swallowing a sword. But then the burning pain subsided, to be followed by a euphoric glow. The sensation was splendid.

"Her color's better now. I think she'll be all right. Why not put her in that chair? It looks comfortable."

Bobby Blessing's voice came from somewhere behind me. Then I was scooped up and rearranged gently in a big leather chair. I was in the library at Tribute, a room that was typically Gull Harbor down to the last piece of hand-rubbed wood paneling: the ubiquitous English hunting prints . . . the ever-present French toile curtains . . . the well-laid fire waiting for the match . . . the leather-topped desk . . . the easy chairs . . . the TV built into the bookcases which themselves were filled with leather-bound volumes in perfect order . . . the bar, cleverly concealed in a niche in the wall. Perfect—everything perfect.

There were, however, two atypical notes to rescue the

18

room from utter banality—a leather-covered chair fashioned from the horns of Texas steers and a buffalo rug, smelling faintly of moth balls. Bobby Blessing was seated in the chair with the rug curling stiffly around his feet. He looked like a cross between a spider—for he was all arms and legs—and a cattle baron.

Actually there was one more thing to save the scene— the man who was now leaning against the bar, which was open, and smiling at me. A man that good looking would save any scene.

"I think you'll live," he said. "He never intended to kill you, or he would have, whoever he was."

"Must have heard us coming down the drive. Took off. Probably down the service road. Left you lying in the front hall. So stupid of you to be here." Bobby Blessing looked crossly at me and my sense of well-being evaporated. It was a little like having the pope displeased. Bobby Blessing had that kind of power.

I suppose he was the most distinguished man in Gull Harbor, where distinguished citizens are anything but a rarity. You could probably say that he was a diplomatic jack-of-all-trades: he'd held three cabinet posts, been advisor to five different presidents, and headed countless special diplomatic missions.

But his power was more subtle than all that. At seventy, he was still in daily touch with Washington, a kind of permanent minister without portfolio to the American government, and his influence seeped into countless secret and unsuspected quarters.

All of this I knew from my aunt, who adored him. I also knew that he was the last man in the world I wanted to be angry with me.

"Whatever made you do such a stupid thing? Why did you come here? Your aunt told you not to, didn't she?"

I tried to think of something intelligent to say and couldn't. Then I tried to say I was sorry. But all that came out was a series of unattractive croaks, like a raven.

19

Blessing's expression softened a little. "There, there . . . don't try to speak. I suppose it was the eternal female curiosity. My wife was like that—couldn't bear not to look into everything—like a cat, you know." He got up—in stages . . . a wooden ruler unfolding. "Well now, Alex, as the young lady's more or less all right, let's get on with what we came here for, shall we?"

The man at the bar nodded and stepped swiftly into the hall and out of sight. It was as if someone had turned out the light, which was strange because his hair was black and his skin was perfectly tanned. Maybe it was the eyes . . . they were very blue. Electric blue.

"Alexander Dana," Blessing told me, as if it explained everything. He began to poke about among the bookshelves.

I produced a croak of interrogation.

"Lawyer fellow with Lassiter's bank. Got a call from Washington last night. Asked me to let him in here today . . . looking for something." I heard the desk drawers being opened.

From my chair beside Lassiter's bar I could see across the hall into the dining room, where Dana now came into view. He was obviously looking for something but no lawyer with a bank ever looked for something the way Dana was doing now. He was unscrewing light bulbs and poking among the fixtures. He was examining the moldings. He was feeling the trompe l'oeil panels with his hands and then scanning them with some sort of instrument. Every movement was swift, light, sure. In the span of only a few minutes he was through and had moved out of sight again into another area.

I got up unsteadily and leaned into the bar, searching for the brandy. Another drop or two might complete the job of anesthetizing my throat . . . I had never yearned more for speech.

Bobby Blessing was rooting about among the fireplace logs, a performance I found absolutely extraordinary in a man of his age and dignity. I discovered the brandy and

20

administered it to myself. The result was miraculous: bits and pieces of my voice were restored.

"Looking for what?" I cried, happy as a diva newly recovered from laryngitis. "They had lots of papers at the meeting this morning outside on the lawn."

"Where, exactly?"

"Off in the far corner."

"So they wouldn't be seen by someone coming to the front door." His voice was grim. "Wasn't a meeting at all. Going over what they found."

My voice was still scratchy and uneven, but it was back in service. "Looking for what?" I repeated, somewhat desperately this time.

"Anything unusual. Anything that doesn't fit the pattern . . . Lassiter's pattern." He was dusting his hands with an immaculate monogrammed handkerchief. His hands were long and bony like the rest of his frame, which itself was a frail monument to enduring ulcers.

Alexander Dana was back in the room, his return swift and silent. I couldn't believe I hadn't noticed him come back, but I hadn't.

"Anything?" he asked Blessing.

"Nothing," Blessing replied. "You?"

"Negative. Cleaned out. Not even a scrap of burned paper. Very professional."

Blessing grunted.

"Drink?" I asked them. They looked so disappointed I wanted to do something to comfort them. They agreed to whiskey and soda, which I fixed. We sat in silence after that, Dana on the corner of the desk, Blessing in the long-horn chair, and me beside the bar. I was longing to ask more questions, but their mood was so black I didn't dare.

Finally their glasses were empty.

"Might as well get going," Blessing said. "You well enough now to go home, Persis?"

I wished that I had the nerve to pretend I was too faint to drive. Then I could request the services of Alexander Dana,

21

who was otherwise about to disappear from my life like the proverbial puff of smoke. A typical Gull Harbor lady would have done it: those women are tigers where men are concerned and they believe in the law of the jungle.

Instead I tried to temporize. "You said anything that doesn't fit the pattern, didn't you? Could it be anything that doesn't fit the pattern of the house?"

"Could be." They both looked at me with interest.

"Well, there are a couple of things. The buffalo rug, for instance."

"Nothing there."

"The chair . . . those horns."

"Obvious. But we checked anyway. Negative."

"The bar."

"The bar?"

I might never have noticed if it hadn't been for the words Marseille and Maures. I knew those places well and my attention was automatically arrested.

"Didn't you see?"

They both came over to the bar and frowned at it. Even when he frowned Dana looked marvelous—a little more dangerous and macho and marvelous.

"It's nothing but wallpaper made from the reproduction of a French newspaper. What's so unusual about that? Every bar and bathroom in Gull Harbor features French wallpaper with smart remarks on it. Who pays any attention? Who, in fact, reads French?"

True enough, the local landscape abounds in examples of French powder room wit—it is the last gasp in chic these days. It is also true that most Gull Harbor men don't know a word of French. They seem to harbor a suspicion that to know French is slightly decadent and best left to the ladies or to hirelings. One of my chief responsibilities at the art gallery where I earn my meager living is to translate all French correspondence for my employer, Gregor Olitsky.

"Well, I read French, and even though the type is so

small as to be nearly indecipherable I can just make it out because I have good eyes. Let me translate.''

And I did.

It was pages one and four of *Le Provençal*, Marseille, reproduced over and over again and set at different angles to make an endless pattern which was tiny but actually very handsome. The *Le Provençal* masthead was in a bright, orangy red and everything else was in black and white. Reading it wasn't easy, but it could be done.

The date was Friday, August 12, 1977.

Page one was ablaze with headlines, all of them celebrating catastrophes:

"Les enquêteurs sur les traces de l'assassin de Monique," screamed one. *"New York respire! Le 'Fils de Sam' enfin arrêté!"* cried another. *"Un réseau de 'traite des blanches' découvert entre la Belgique et le Midi. Quatre arrestations,"* proclaimed a third.

One headline was special because the story pertaining to it took up most of page four. LE DOUBLE CRIME DU MASSIF PRÈS DES MAURES . . . LES PISTES S'EFFONDRENT UNE À UNE.

The entire center of page four concerned itself with this story, so prominently headlined on the front page. Under the great black headline, LA FORÊT DES MAURES GARDE SON SECRET, there was a four column report of the deaths by gunfire (*"froidement tués à coups de revolver"*) of two British citizens, Mr. and Mrs. Broderick-Smith, found dead beside their Ford Cortina. The colonel in charge of the investigation was quoted as stating that robbery was not necessarily the motive for the crime. There were no clues— no record of the Broderick-Smith's activities before their deaths, although it was assumed that they were on a camping vacation. London was quoted as saying that neither of the deceased had any family. There was a rumor that Scotland Yard was sending an investigator. A witness was quoted as having seen two motorcyclists near the scene of the crime, which took place in an area where the terrain was much favored by the fans of *"la moto verte."* The

23

witness confessed that the two motorcyclists would be impossible to identify since they were wearing helmets and the typical leather garb of their genre.

I had glanced at this lead story in a purely cursory way, thinking to myself that it was an odd sort of thing to reproduce in wallpaper and deciding that the left hand side of the page, which contained a detailed account of the arrest of the mad killer known as Son of Sam, was probably the reason for the bizarre choice. A lot of people had followed the Son of Sam story—maybe Lassiter thought it made an amusing conversation piece for his bar. Gull Harbor is high on conversation pieces.

But when I happened to look at the headline beneath the story on the two murders in the hills of Maures, I was startled . . . and fascinated. While the two men searched the house around me, I read it through twice.

First the headline caught my attention. DES SIMILITUDES TROUBLANTES, it announced. And the similarities listed below could indeed be called troubling.

Between the years 1952 and 1977 no fewer than eight British citizens had been murdered within the roughly triangular area that joined Marseille, Menton, and Manosque. In 1952 Sir James Drumm and his wife were assassinated near Lurs and the case was still considered extremely controversial. In 1964 another representative of *"L'Establishment Britannique,"* Sir Duncan Oliver, was shot in Cannes, where he had lived during the Second World War. In 1973 the body of Jeremy Michael, a British officer in retirement, was discovered on the Promenade des Anglais in Nice. Two months later John Cartland Basil, another British subject, was found assassinated near Pelissanne. In 1975 Prentice Courtney, ex-RAF pilot, was found murdered in Menton. Finally, the deaths of the Broderick-Smiths.

The crimes, the news story reported, had many points in common:

1. All of the victims were British.
2. All the men belonged to the same generation, rang-

24

ing from sixty-one to seventy-five years of age.

3. All had been involved in World War II.

4. All were very familiar with the southeast of France . . . one lived there (Michael) . . . one was born there (Oliver) . . . the others had been coming to the area over a great number of years (Drumm, Basil, Broderick-Smith, Courtney).

5. During the war, Sir Duncan Oliver had directed, from Cannes, an important branch of the affiliated Resistance. Jeremy Michael had worked directly with him. Basil had been attached to the S.O.E., the special British branch of the service operating in France in very close association with some of the principal branches of the Resistance. According to British authorities, Sir James Drumm had not played "any particular role" during the war—yet he was knighted by King George VI for *"services rendus au titre du ministère du Ravitaillement."* As to Prentice Courtney, "ex-RAF pilot," killed at Menton, he would have been forty-two years old in 1942—an age when one no longer piloted Spitfires and Mosquitos. Why then, was he identified by Britain as an RAF pilot?

Was it not possible, the story demanded, that Drumm, Oliver, Michael, Basil, Courtney, and Broderick-Smith were all killed for the same reason . . . and by the same assassin?

"Alors," the writer concluded cryptically, *"roman policier? Voire. . . ."*

Blessing and Dana listened to my reading of the material with fierce concentration, Blessing hum, humming to himself, Dana in silence. I re-read it several times. It seemed a very long time before they spoke . . . the power of their concentration was such that I would not have been astonished if the newsprint had leapt off the wall.

"That's it," Dana said, finally turning away. "If he had any detailed . . . ." He seemed to have dismissed the wallpaper. ". . . but I seriously doubt that he committed anything to writing . . . he was too professional for that."

25

"Agreed." Blessing came over and put his arm around me in what I suppose was a gesture of affection, although it felt more as if someone had dropped a bundle of sharp sticks onto my shoulders. "Well, well. Very original—very amusing. But we've come away empty-handed. Very clever of Lassiter, actually. Very. Poor bastard."

I looked from one to the other. "Clever?"

"Well, certainly different. A sort of 'lest we forget old British heroes' every time he mixed a drink. There must have been others since that was written."

Dana didn't look pleased and I thought I heard him mutter "stupidity" beneath his breath but I wasn't sure.

"Of course," Blessing continued, "Lassiter always was a conceited ass. I hate to admit it, but it's true. Always thought the British were smarter—that *he* was smarter than anyone else—thumbing his nose. Really believed he was superior, like all those Brits."

It seemed to be a total non sequitur, much more worthy of my aunt than of Bobby Blessing. I decided to ignore it. "You said you're coming away empty-handed. What exactly are you. . . ."

"Just couldn't resist, could he?" Blessing was talking over me at Dana and this time I distinctly heard Dana say, "Stupid."

It was too much. My frustration made my voice rise half an octave.

"Well, there's one thing you must know . . . why are you calling Courtney Lassiter a poor bastard? Why?"

This time they answered.

"Because he's dead, Persis." There was a kind of rage in Blessing. "Dead. He was found on the Boulevard Canebière in Marseille."

"Yesterday morning," said Dana.

The triangle joining Marseille, Menton, and Manosque.

"Oh, no." Dead in Marseille.

One corner of the triangle.

"He was shot eight times at close range."

26

"Like an assassination!"

"Like an execution." Dana's voice had a January chill.

Blessing shrugged. "That's the way punks operate today. Kill you for a dime. In any case—dead. We're trying to find some necessary papers. A will. All that. And by the way, we'd appreciate it if you didn't say anything about his being dead. Not just yet, please. No one even knows he was in France and there are details to be worked out. Better not have everyone thrashing about—until we find the will and his other papers, that is. Agreed?"

"Agreed." A will, maybe. Important papers, definitely. And it was a safe bet that Blessing and Dana weren't the only ones looking: Godzilla and I must have jumped right into the middle of a search. "But as I seem to be an unwitting participant in this affair, couldn't you give me some idea of what it's all about?"

"Don't know ourselves." Bobby had the grace not to look me in the eye as he said it: he was obviously lying.

"Sorry. We can't." Dana was at least polite.

"Oh," I said.

There didn't seem to be anything else to say.

As it turned out, I did not drive myself home. Dana drove me, but it wasn't to my house, where there was some slight chance I could invent a delaying action that would hold him in place while I got to know him better. It was instead, after a brief conference with Blessing and a hushed telephone call by the latter to someone who could only have been my aunt, back to The Crossing.

"Your car will be picked up by one of the chauffeurs and returned to your house. You're in no condition to drive yourself. And you ought to be at your aunt's where you will be properly looked after until you recover." This was Blessing.

"But all I have is a sore throat. I can look after myself perfectly well."

27

"Absolutely not. In these incidents there is always danger of delayed shock."

"My housekeeper, Mrs. Howard. . . ."

"She's not there at night, is she? No—it's The Crossing. Your aunt won't hear of anything else. Anyway, she thinks you need to be fed."

And The Crossing it was.

Three

My esteemed aunt, Lydia Wentworth, is a famous lady.

Not that she wants to be. In fact her one proclaimed desire in life is to be anonymous.

"A lady's name appears in the press on only three occasions," she is fond of announcing, ". . . when she is born . . . when she is married . . . and when she dies."

By those standards, as she is now in her dazzlingly handsome mid-sixties, her name should have appeared twice: on the occasions of her birth and her marriage. But she has never married and I think she never will, although she views men with undisguised enthusiasm. She is afraid, I am persuaded, that men wish to marry her for her very impressive fortune.

In actual fact and to her horror her name is in the papers all the time. She complains that she can't understand it, but everyone else can. She's one of the wealthiest women in the world. She's beautiful. She has an opulent life style. Fabulous jewels. Houses around the world. The oldest limousine in captivity and a world-famous art collection.

But in her mind's eye, she is just a simple person living

28

a simple life and doing charitable works when she can. I, Persis Willum, have come under the heading of charitable works ever since I was ten years old and my parents had the misfortune to vanish at sea while cruising the Bahamas.

"Most unfortunate," said my aunt and proceeded to do her duty, shepherding me into adulthood, albeit from a more-or-less safe distance. "I find children alarming," she confessed; and sentenced me to boarding schools round the clock—a sentence sweetened, when she felt particularly robust, by occasional trips to the races in England or Normandy and house parties with assorted nobility in the south of France. "It is important for a young girl to learn the amenities," she had said, and taught me to ride sidesaddle, to curtsy to grownups and, after I was sixteen, to drink a "brut" champagne from the proper flute and to distinguish between a Bordeaux and a Burgundy.

It was an interesting education and I adored her.

An interesting education. Except that she didn't educate me about men. "They're lovely," was all she ever said on the subject.

So at eighteen I married and educated myself.

And by the time he had drunk his way through my modest inheritance and into the grave I knew all I wanted to know: namely that it's all right to fall in love but marriage is dangerous. At thirty-six I have occasional attacks of falling in love, but not many. My luck has not been good, my record has not been shining, and my choices have not been enviable.

"You really ought to marry again," my aunt is always saying, which isn't fair considering her own antipathy to the marital state.

Lydia Wentworth is quixotic. I long ago resigned myself to the fact that she has one set of rules for herself and a completely different set for the rest of the world. "You're not bad looking, my dear, particularly now and then." And she would shake her silver cap of platinum hair, flash her

29

jewels, and gaze at me with momentary interest before going off on an entirely different subject.

It was like Beauty telling the Beast to have hope. Although actually I'm not that bad. I'm medium tall and medium blond and there's nothing wrong with my legs, I'm told. In fact, there are days when construction workers and men in manholes carry on wildly.

I scratch out a sort of living by running Gregor Olitsky's chain of art galleries and selling an occasional painting of my own. I have a car and a house and Mrs. Howard to clean it and that's about all. In fact, I *like* my little house and I *like* my little life and my reaction to the prospect of a sojourn at The Crossing was comparable to that of the peasant being dragged into the palace and ordered to enjoy it.

But I was here and there was nothing to do but surrender joyously to my fate.

As fates go, it was strictly first class. The minute I set foot in the great hall I found myself coddled and pampered and fed quantities of throat-soothing honey from The Crossing's own hives and plied, between times, with quantities of fine food and drink.

My arrogant cat, Isadore Duncan (so named by my housekeeper, Mrs. Howard, a notorious nonspeller, because "she's always jumpin' around") had come along with me and she took to her new life like a duck to water. In short order she had the servants enslaved and Aunt Lydie's myriad small dogs subjugated.

I, too, was seduced by my surroundings. Was I under house arrest? Had Blessing ordered Aunt Lydie to keep me out of his hair? It didn't matter—the hot-and-cold-running service and free-flowing luxury were wildly appealing. Being poor may be good for the creative juices, as starving artists have bravely maintained, but a short wallow in luxury is good for everything else.

There were also great quantities of vintage champagne to seal my fate.

"So good for the health," my aunt said.

"Which?"

"All of it."

And she was right. I prospered.

Roberts reported with horror that my car was in desperate need of a complete overhaul. Happily, I gave him permission to take it apart. Why would I need a car when I was perfectly content to stay where I was?

Blessing and Dana hadn't totally abandoned me. Occasionally they appeared like twin visions bearing photographs for me to examine. Aunt Lydie always absented herself on these occasions. She detested unpleasantness of any kind: when faced with anything disagreeable she simply ignored it.

The attack on me had been disagreeable.

The photographs Dana and Blessing produced at regular intervals were always of oriental types. They looked more or less alike to me. I could identify none of them.

"I'm sorry. I'm not good at oriental types. And anyway, I was mostly interested in the telephone pole and the garden and his nonfitting coat."

"Don't be absurd, Persis. Lydia keeps talking about your 'artist's eye.' Let's see it." Blessing was accepting no excuses. As usual.

Dana was nicer.

In fact he was very nice.

Nicer with every passing day. He even turned up now and then without Blessing. There was always a good reason . . . more photographs, a question to be answered.

He rarely spoke. He didn't have to. I found myself, rasping less and less, talking my head off. I chattered away about everything imaginable. And he listened with grave courtesy as if he had a serious concern for every word I spoke. It was very flattering.

Courtesy—he was old-fashioned about that. And when he smiled it was like a gift.

At the same time there was something about him that

31

was unreachable. There was a reserve that attracted me; I kept wanting to find the person beneath the person I saw every day. I sensed fire. But I never saw it. He was always unruffled and composed and yes, a little cold.

But I didn't believe that he was really cold. He was complex—that was it. Unfathomable. Little hints of another person kept flickering through the dispassionate surface.

I'm Aries; and Aries is always seduced by the unanswered question. Heedless, headstrong Aries.

If I ever wondered why an estate lawyer had the time to linger at Gull Harbor and The Crossing, I didn't wonder much. I was too happy to have him around.

You're not falling in love, I told myself sternly.

As if I wasn't.

 *Four*

Within a few days Blessing and Dana arrived with a photograph I *could* identify.

I looked at it once and nearly toppled over. There was no mistaking this oriental gentleman: I felt my throat begin to swell, my voice begin to disappear. I was back at Lassiter's front door with unrelenting hands gripping me.

"He's the one."

Dana and Blessing, those two specimens of super-cool, suddenly lit up. Blessing almost allowed himself to smile; Dana's India sapphire eyes shot out beams of light.

"Persis, are you sure?"

"I'm absolutely certain. Who is he?"

32

"Nobody you'd invite to tea."

"I could guess that much. But exactly who is he? I think I'm entitled to know: I've been shot at and nearly strangled during this affair."

"It will be better for you the less you know."

I felt my temper rising. "I am not a child. You insult me."

So they offered a soupçon. "All we know about him is that he was formerly a member of something called the Mitzu Brigade."

"I never heard of it."

"Not surprising. It's one of those obscure terrorist groups."

"Is that all you're going to tell me?" Apparently it was, but I couldn't accept a lone crumb—I wanted the whole cake. I had an idea. "Does this have anything to do with the article last month in the *Gull Harbor Trumpet?*"

"*Trumpet?* Good Lord, Persis—who reads the *Trumpet?*"

"Well, I do and maybe you should."

"Are you serious? What article are you talking about?"

"An article warning us that there had been a rash of international bank hold-ups and kidnappings for money which Interpol expects to spread to the USA. Somebody's trying to raise huge sums of money and the *Trumpet* was warning Gull Harbor's millionaires to guard their flanks. Terrorists, they said."

They were silent.

"What were you doing—really doing—at Lassiter's the day you rescued me? Why won't you say? What was a member of the Mitzu Brigade doing there? What *is* the Mitzu Brigade? Who is doing what to whom and why?"

Dana picked up the photograph. "Thank you for letting us annoy you with this."

Bobby began the slow rise from his chair, section by long, brittle section. Either he or the chair creaked slightly. "Damn lucky for us you have a good eye, Persis."

33

"But—"

Once again it was no use.

"We must rush off, my dear. Sorry."

And that's exactly what they did. I felt like a spanked child—one who might burst into tears of rage and disappointment at any moment.

Five

The next day they were back. This time it was at my request.

Aunt Lydie and Isadore Duncan and I were just finishing luncheon. It was after the salmon soufflé and the fresh peaches. Actually, Isadore was still picking delicately at her soufflé, which had been served to her on one of the best china plates and placed on the floor next to the white wicker basket-bed Aunt Lydie had bought her and which she refused to set foot in—she was a tabletop cat.

Gull Harbor mail is delivered to the front door by a lady who drives a red, white, and blue jeep and is extremely polite. Nobody keeps a mailbox anymore—there's too much vandalism by people who drive out to Long Island to vent their resentment of the rich by smashing mailboxes.

Today she was later than usual and it wasn't until after our coffee was served that Jennings appeared with the mail on a silver tray.

There was one letter for me. It was covered with colorful stamps and the return address was Sir Courtney Lassiter, Tribute, Gull Harbor, N.Y. USA 11771.

I reached instantly for the telephone. "Bobby—there's something here. I need you at once."

"Of course. What is it, Persis?"

"A letter."

"Yes?" A mere letter obviously did not alarm him.

"It's from Courtney Lassiter and it's addressed to me. Bobby—he's been dead for days."

"Hang on, Persis—I'll be right there."

I can't open it—I just can't." Even I could hear the hysteria in my voice.

For once Blessing was sympathetic. "Of course you can't. Damn the mails, anyway. I'll get Dana and we'll be right there."

He was as good as his word.

"It's the mails," Blessing repeated reassuringly when they arrived, slightly breathless. "They've gone to hell all over the world. It's everywhere—especially France. He must have mailed it the day they . . . the day he died. You did the right thing in calling us. Now don't you worry. We'll take care of everything." He took the letter from me. I hadn't even realized I was still holding it.

Dana made comforting rumbles. I wanted to bury my head in his shoulder and close my eyes but I didn't think he'd permit it. So I kept my eyes on Blessing. Still wearing driving gloves, he was holding the letter and slitting it carefully with a silver fruit knife he had taken from the luncheon table. How meticulous he is, I thought dully.

He read the letter several times. Then he passed it to Dana. Dana was equally meticulous: he held it by the corner with his white handkerchief. Did they really hope to pick up fingerprints after all the people who had handled it?

I began to feel well enough, now that they had opened the letter, to be curious. "What does it say?"

Dana shook his head. "We'll check for prints to be sure it's genuine. . . ."

Blessing followed up. "Strange sort of thing for Lassiter

35

to do. First of all, why write you? Second, the message . . . it's scarcely his sort of thing. Wants to know about a certain . . . what exactly does he say?—'street photographer' of the nineteen thirties. A man named Praha. 'Very obscure,' he says. Long before your time, Persis—that's what's odd. Says he was obscure. Nothing in the books about him.''

They stood there and looked at me, Bobby very tweedy and country squire-ish and Dana very knock-you-dead in an open blue shirt and blue sweater exactly the color of his eyes.

''Well, you are something of an art scholar,'' Dana said finally. ''I suppose you might know—or at least be able to find out.''

Blessing continued to eye me speculatively. ''I suppose it could be genuine, although God knows it's atypical as all hell. Ever heard of this what's-his-name—Praha fellow?''

''No.'' If God was ever going to strike me dead, now was the time.

They continued to stare at me—two men who had asked a question of what they considered a sort of two-legged art computer and trustfully, confidently, expected it to spit out an answer.

''Sure?''

''Certain. The letter must be a fake.''

''*Sure* you don't know this fellow—Praha?''

''I'm sure. It would have been before I was born and, anyway, photography is not my field. Never heard anything about him.''

It was only a little lie. I knew nothing about Praha, but I had heard his name.

It was the kind of name one remembered.

''Could I?'' I reached for the letter.

They didn't give it to me. Instead, Blessing put it carefully in his coat pocket, handling it fastidiously with his gloved hand. ''Sorry, Persis. You understand.''

36

I understood, all right. I understood that it was the last straw. Once again Blessing and Mr. Alexander-Mysterious-Dana were insisting on telling me nothing, even though I was the one who had been shot at and strangled. They wouldn't tell me about the terrorists and now they wouldn't even let me see my own letter—the letter that was sent to *me*. Did they think I was incapable of handling the information?

Yes, I understood. I understood that they were shutting me out again. Once too often.

I'm not the type to make a passive victim: I take a very dim view of being shot at and strangled.

"I understand." I understood that I now had two scraps of information which they did not have. They believed we were the only ones who had known Lassiter was in the south of France. They did not read the *Trumpet*. An oversight. *Someone* knew. And they did not know about Praha.

I had two small scraps—very small. But I was going to run with them. I owed it to myself.

Then I remembered that my car was out of commission. I'd have to talk someone into giving me a ride to the gallery. I'd talk Gregor's alcoholic secretary, Withers, into letting me borrow the gallery van.

And run.

Maybe I'd tell Bobby and Dana later.

Maybe I wouldn't.

Six

The first thing I did after I picked up the van (Withers, rattling her beads in the closet where she kept her favorite brand of Scotch, hadn't even noticed me take the keys), was to call Ed Simms at his dingy institutional green office at the FBI. Or maybe it was puce: the paint was so old one couldn't really tell.

Simms was an old friend. I'd once helped him uncover a treasure trove of missing masterpieces and he owed me, as they say.

He wasn't there. Naturally. No one in New York is ever there the first time you call.

So I headed for the *Gull Harbor Trumpet*. The *Trumpet* was a pretty quiet place except on Mondays, when they typed up the newspaper and put it to bed. Two harried and vastly underpaid local housewives batted out almost the entire six-page weekly single-handed. The truth is, they were more like martyrs than housewives: they even solicited and pasted up the ads. The only things they didn't do were the so-called society column and the editorials. These were produced by the Editor-and-Publisher.

Today happened to be Wednesday. A citizen burning to present the *Trumpet* with news of an ax murder would either have to push a note under the door (no one answered the bell) or find a phone booth and telephone. In the latter case he would be forced to leave a message on an answering machine. "This is your local newspaper, the *Gull Harbor Trumpet*, Long Island's best. If you have a message for us, begin speaking when you hear the tone and we will get back to you at our earliest convenience."

I, however, was not misled by any of this. Light years ago, in an idle moment, I had written an art column for the *Trumpet* and I was therefore familiar with the Inner Workings, unanswered door bells and answering machines notwithstanding.

What I knew that nobody else knew was that the Editor-and-Publisher was in there tending her clippings, and tending them with all the loving care great gardeners lavish on their gardens.

The clippings were her personal religion. With fearsome dedication she combed, day after day, *The New York Times*, the *Daily News*, the *New York Post*, the *International Herald Tribune*, the *Wall Street Journal*, the *Cleveland Plain Dealer*—everything she could lay her hands on in the way of a major publication, many of them foreign, searching for things that might have a Gull Harbor point of view. It made the *Trumpet* seem terribly *au courant*. As a result *The New York Times*, the *News*, the Post, the *International Herald Tribune*, and the *Wall Street Journal* also combed the *Trumpet*'s pages for items they could rewrite from *their* point of view. After all, some of the most newsworthy persons in the world lived in Gull Harbor or its environs. The only difference was that it didn't take them as long to browse through the six-page *Trumpet*.

Her name was Kate Cochran, but she answered only to Cochran; and she was right where I knew she'd be—in her office, clipping items.

Cochran was not your average Gull Harborite. For one thing, although she was still handsome, she was the only person in a community of immaculate dressers who always looked as if she had never quite managed to get to bed all week, let alone to change her clothes. For another, while guarding the honor of Gull Harbor and its citizens with a loyalty bordering on the fanatic, she was gleefully irreverent toward those same citizens, chastising them in print

39

and to their faces with a lack of respect that only a peer would dare employ.

"You must understand Cochran," people said, forgiving her. "She was briefly at school in Paris in the thirties—the Sorbonne—and she fell in with Gertrude Stein and that crowd and turned into a sort of precursor of today's Hippies."

"Sure I met Stein," she would answer. "I was invited to her salons a couple of times—met Hemingway, Braque. She thought I was cute. But I was just a kid, for God's sake. I can hardly remember her . . . or them." She had never married although she had a lovely long body and a marvelously sculptured head and nose and an El Greco kind of special good looks.

She was sitting today at a desk that was approximately the size of a map table in a war room, every inch of the surface smothered in half empty Coke bottles and papers of one kind or another. When she saw me in the doorway she shoved her glasses up into the unkempt turmoil of her hair and smiled with undisguised pleasure.

"Persis!" Gesturing with a huge pair of library scissors. "Come sit down. Where have you been hiding?" For some reason Cochran had always liked me. I suspect that she considered me a fellow Bohemian.

She pushed back from her desk and emptied an overflowing ashtray into the metal scrap basket beside her desk. "What's up?"

A wisp of smoke rose immediately from the scrap basket and without even taking her eyes from me she reached for an open Coke bottle and emptied it on the would-be conflagration. The smoke subsided instantly.

"I need to know who told you Sir Courtney Lassiter was in the south of France." With Cochran it was best to be direct. She did not like to waste time.

"Lassiter?" She ran her fingers through her exuberant gray-blond curls until she found one lock of hair that was too long. Without hesitation she clipped it off and dropped

40

it in the scrap basket. "You, too, Persis? I didn't know you were attracted to older men. All the widows and divorcées in Gull Harbor have been calling me for weeks asking where he is."

"I'm not attracted to older men."

"Then there must be a story in it. Promise to let me have it first." She studied me with deepening interest. "What could it be about, I wonder? Well, never mind— you'll tell me when you're ready, I trust."

I laughed. "At this moment, it's just personal curiosity." Trying to sound a bit mysterious.

"All right—I won't press. Let's see—I log every call I use in the column. Self protection. It was Nadia Milonsky—here it is. She didn't say it was confidential. I'd called to ask if she'd give me an interview and if it was true she was doing a portrait of the president—remember, he'd just turned down somebody else's?"

He said it belonged in a home for the blind. "Yes."

"The bit about Lassiter just slipped out. She asked me not to mention the presidential business, but said nothing about Lassiter. Inferred I might have an interview if I didn't use it during her lifetime."

"Typical."

"I remember now. She wouldn't discuss the president but she said she was working on four new portraits."

"I didn't see their names in your column."

"No. Same thing. Feels that they might not want their names in print. Everyone's scared of being kidnapped."

It was true: none but the super-rich could afford a Milonsky portrait. A Milonsky likeness on the wall was proof of having arrived, socially and financially.

"Who? Telling me isn't the same as having it in print. I'd love to know."

"Why not? No harm in it. All she mentioned was not having it in print. The whole community probably knows by now."

"I'm always the last to know."

41

"Me, too." She offered me a newly opened Coke and when I declined, drank it herself. I waited patiently.

"It's always like that," she continued finally. "People swear me to secrecy and then I find out the whole world's been publishing it. Well, here it is."

She scribbled down four names and handed them to me. I read the list. "They have one thing in common—they're pretty international."

"*Everybody* in Gull Harbor is international."

"They're all more or less newcomers."

She sighed. "Everybody else has already been painted by Milonsky. She runs through millionaires the way Montezuma's Revenge runs through Mexican tourists. It's like the great society photographers in the forties and fifties. If you're not 'done,' you haven't arrived."

"Speaking of photographers . . . do you remember when we were planning an exhibition of twentieth-century photographers at the gallery? We never got our act together, but while we were considering it I called you for advice?" Cochran was a gifted and highly skilled press photographer. It was how she had started out with the New York dailies before her family bought her the foundering *Gull Harbor Trumpet* to play with. She seldom bothered with photography today—she had slaves to do that, freelance.

"At the North Shore Galleries? I remember."

"And you said we must not overlook a French photographer of the thirties named Praha?"

"The 'lost photographer.' I remember."

"You said I must try to find his book, *Parisian Nights.*"

"They talked about him at Gertrude Stein's. They were all crazy for anything new. And they couldn't stand it because nobody knew who he was. They had to know everything and everyone, otherwise what use is it to be the avant-garde?"

"What did they say?"

"He was a genius. Prowled the streets of Paris by night,

42

taking pictures of prostitutes, pimps, and criminals at work.''

"You remember all this?"

"Of course—even then I had a nose for a story." She clipped off another curl—frowning, distracted, remembering. "He published a book, *Parisian Nights,* and before anything but a few critics' copies reached the public the publisher's warehouse burned down. Then Praha's studio caught fire and the original glass plates were destroyed. You can imagine that Stein's circle would have sold their souls to see a copy: everyone was buzzing.''

"You saw the book?"

"No one saw it that I know of.''

"Do you think it was destroyed on purpose?"

"Parisians love to talk. Their version was—and they also love *l'amour*—that a society lady visited the Paris *boites* for amusement . . . it was la mode in those days. She met a pretty young man in one of the bistros and there was an affair. She did not know that he was a petty criminal—he said he was a sculptor's assistant and maybe he was that, too. One day he tried to blackmail her—either she pay him what he asked or he would tell the husband. When she threatened to go to the police, he killed her and her two children. Then he decamped with her jewels and someone began the campaign to destroy *Parisian Nights.*''

I was watching her: she had lit two cigarettes and stubbed them both out after a couple of puffs. Now she coughed, the racking, phlegmy cough of the smoking addict.

When the seizure had passed she continued, gasping a little. "There could only be one reason, we decided at Stein's . . . there must be a photograph in that book of Praha's by which the petty criminal could be identified as a murderer of women and children.''

"What happened?"

"Nothing. Except the war. It came. Praha disappeared. Nothing was ever the same.''

Cochran felt around for her glasses and put them back

43

down on her nose. She picked up a copy of this morning's *Times*. "Anything else?"

"No. Thanks."

"My pleasure." She began to clip, the long silver blades slashing swiftly through the newsprint. "Just remember, I get first crack at any story."

"I'll remember."

It seemed a safe enough promise to make.

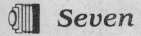 ## Seven

I tried Ed Simms again after I left the *Trumpet*. I called from the telephone booth at the service station on Bay Boulevard and this time he was in.

"I need something, Ed."

He sighed. Everyone was sighing at me today. It made me feel unpopular. "Any use asking you why?"

"Not really. Just take it on faith."

"I suppose it's something you needed to know yesterday?"

"Approximately. But don't worry, it's nothing confidential."

"Oh? That would be a change, at least." He sounded weary. But then he always sounded weary. "What now?"

I had a mental image of him slouched over his desk, running his fingers through the short blondish stubble of his crew cut. He was the only man I knew who still wore his hair short. He would be in a gray suit. He was always in a gray suit. And his brown shoes would have thick crepe soles. They always did.

44

"Nothing much—nothing that will get you fired, anyway. I just want to know if any of the following citizens is Public Enemy Number One." I didn't know very much about Milonsky's new clients. Maybe one of them was bad news. Maybe one of them had known Lassiter and ordered his assassination. After all, they were people who might well be familiar with the Marseille-Menton-Manosque triangle. I rattled off my list and added Nadia Milonsky for good measure: it was she who had actually told Cochran that Lassiter was in the south of France.

There was a pause. Then Simms sighed again. "All right, if that's all you want I'll run it through the computer. It will take a minute. I'll call you back. Where are you calling from?"

I gave him the number. "There's one more thing, Ed."

"There always is," he said resignedly.

"Something called the Mitzu Brigade . . . is it some kind of Japanese chowder and marching club?"

He came to life. The line between us crackled with sudden energy. "Hardly, Persis. Don't mess with those boys: their business is kidnapping and murder. Why are you asking?"

"People keep mentioning them. And are you serious—murder?"

"Never more so. They started out as a few Japanese experts in the oriental arts of killing. Now we believe they're a highly trained coalition of murderers from all over—a super death squad—serving a world network of terrorist groups. They're trained in Bulgaria . . . we think by the KGB, but we have no proof. Have you read the *Times* today?"

The question surprised me. "Not yet." My mind had been on other things.

"Then let me read you an item." I heard the rustle of papers. "Here it is. Page four. Headline: 'DUTCH MILLIONAIRE KIDNAPPED ON AMSTERDAM STREET.' The story says, 'Three people kidnapped the chairman of the giant Heikel

45

oil refineries as he walked to his limousine tonight, the police reported. The officers said the abductors pushed him into an orange van and sped away. The kidnappers fell on Ryhs Heikel, fifty-nine years old, about seven P.M. as he left his office.' There are more details, Persis. I'll skip those. But the last paragraph is significant. 'Two other major kidnappings have occurred in the Netherlands within the last three months. One tycoon was freed upon payment of a $4.3 million ransom, the other upon the payment of $8 million. There have been similar kidnappings in other western European countries in recent months. A special terrorist team is believed to be behind them, although no one has claimed the responsibility.' End of quote, Persis.''

I didn't like the sudden pain I felt in my stomach. ''Fund raising?''

''Exactly.''

''By the Mitzu Brigade?''

''Or a section of it, working for a terrorist alliance called the Coalition.''

''How do you know?''

''We have our informants. We know how it works.''

''How?''

''It's sad. I mean, the way they're recruited. Often they're idealists, believe it or not. *'Entre dans la lutte armée,'* they're told, 'and you will know adventures and women and violence and class war and the *grands hotels.'* Often it is the 'class war' that attracts them, especially if they are students, or poor.''

The man who tried to strangle me—a student? Anything was possible. ''What happens to them?''

''It is a long apprenticeship. They must give up everyone they know and love . . . everything. Their values are tested and changed. And it is a boring, painful process. They are always tested, watched, assessed. And finally, if he is judged good enough to serve, the recruit is placed in contact with a 'regular.' The executive committee will then decide in what capacity he will serve.''

46

"It all sounds very exact."

"All very military. And for the elite . . . the truly gifted and dedicated . . . the Mitzu squad. There will be months of special training. Languages. Professions—cover professions. Weapons. Sten guns . . . Beretta 95Ss . . . 375s . . . Tokarevs . . . bombs. There are specialists in aircraft, missiles, ships, security. By the time they're through training, they wouldn't hesitate to kill their own mothers. The Coalition has one declared objective: to upset the balance of power in the world. That requires funds—mainly to buy arms. *'Chercher l'argent'* is their main occupation and the Brigade is their main tool—through murder for pay, kidnappings."

"Could any members of the Mitzu Brigade be in the United States?" I knew they could: I'd met one. But I asked anyway.

"You bet they could." All of Simms's weary indifference was gone. "We're one hundred percent sure. We believe they have agents here staking out likely kidnap possibilities. We're taking all possible preventive measures. But if they succeed, we'll be forced to advise for the first time in history that the ransom be paid: Italy lost three prominent men by not getting up the ransom on time, England lost a member of the House of Lords. They're killers. Ruthless."

"And what about assassinations? There's been a rash of them. Minor figures to begin with—NATO and Common Market officials, generals, government officials. Car bombings. Shootings. I've been reading the papers. Will it start here now?"

There was a pause. Good old Ed Simms. Careful. Honest. Stodgy. Incorruptible. Then: "We live in bad times, Persis. Sometimes I think morality is dead."

I knew what he meant because I knew Ed Simms. I also knew he was saying that he did expect it to start here.

"The computer, Ed?" There was no use asking him any more questions.

47

"I'll get back to you in a few minutes."

"I'll be waiting."

We were both too depressed by our conversation to say anything more.

While I waited for the pay phone to ring I thought about the first time I had heard Praha's name.

Last year.

It was at the time of the annual art auction on our one and only Gull Harbor educational television channel, channel 21.

Every year all of us in Gull Harbor work for it as volunteers, cajoling and threatening everyone we know into giving up their old china and moose heads and bric-a-brac and treasured bibelots for the benefit of 21. Afterward we help sell the same things on camera.

I hate to think of the number of artists and collectors I have browbeaten into donating to the cause. And, while there are fantastic bargains to be had, I am perfectly sure that some day the Almighty will punish me for the glowing things I have said on the air about certain objects thrust upon me willy-nilly to sell to the highest bidder.

That year I was squeezed onto a folding chair in an anteroom awaiting my turn on camera. All around was a scene of semi-controlled madness. Cameramen were suspended from the ceiling . . . crew members and aides crawled about on hands and knees to avoid being caught on camera . . . principals struggled not to become entangled in cables and equipment. Paintings appeared on the monitors upside down. Occasional passing legs received star billing. Names and copy were now and then transposed, with hilarious results.

The anteroom was even more chaotic than the studio itself. All about me, like flotsam clinging to the sides of a dock, were deer heads, floor lamps, roll-top desks, jardiniers, spitoons, umbrella stands, pottery dogs, batik wall hangings, mysterious sculptures, Chinese bowls, outsize

48

paintings, nineteenth-century bronzes, and hundreds of other fascinating items.

I sat with my feet jammed in among boxes of donations and prayed that I would be asked to auction something I wouldn't have to lie about.

And that's when I heard Praha's name.

"The sons of bitches sold the Praha book," someone said.

I turned my head. Two disheveled men in shirt sleeves—volunteers—were leaning among the odds and ends behind me drinking Sprite from cans.

"I thought you were going to bid on it?" Vaguely interested.

"I was. Did you see it? No? Praha was some photographer. Artistic, you know. But the insides of brothels and all that. I tell you—great. Paris. Those women. . . ." Eyes brightening. "Came in with a bunch of stuff from some rich old recluse . . . you know, the one that died last year. There aren't supposed to be any copies left."

"So what happened?"

"They got a telephone bid before it came up . . . for so much money they couldn't refuse and they let it go. The one condition was that the guy remain anonymous."

"So you can't buy it back."

"That's right. Couldn't afford it anyway, from what I hear."

"Tough luck."

"You said it! It was some book."

And that was the first time I heard Praha's name.

Cochran had been the second.

The telephone in the street-side booth jangled right on schedule. I leapt out of the van where I had been waiting and answered by the fourth ring.

"Persis?" He sounded a little more cheerful. "No Public Enemy Number One on your list—sorry. But I can't say they're solid citizens because, except for Milonsky, none is a citizen yet."

49

I guess I was relieved. "Could you run them down for me? Remember, you owe me."

"No harm. You probably know it all anyway. Let's see . . . Marcel Martin is French. Made his fortune in pornographic films—you didn't know that, I suspect. Officially, he advertises himself as a producer of art films. You don't care where they were born and all that . . . just bare facts, right? Unmarried. Takes his yacht to France every summer. Wants to become an American citizen."

Martin. I'd seen him around. Typical small Frenchman. Attractive enough. "Art films? Well, well. Next?"

"Hans von Berger. Buys and sells aircraft around the world. Makes tons of money. Supplies Third World countries. Probably makes crooked deals but no overt dishonesty apparent."

Von Berger. One of those blond German gods. The hit of Gull Harbor society. He and Martin both had the hostesses in a flaming flap. Von Berger stood out in any crowd. But Martin was no slouch either—both were marvelous at kissing the hand without actually touching it.

"Hallsey Bryce," Simms went on. "He's supposed to be an inventor but no one has ever seen visible proof of anything he invented. English. Rolling in money. Must be at least seventy years old. His wife's about fifty years younger. French."

Bryce. A brutal looking, glowering sort of man with a pretty child-wife trotting from party to party at his heels. I'd met the whole list here and there at this or that party.

"And Milonsky?" I asked.

"Countess Milonsky, if you please. Claims to be Russian aristocracy—the woods are full of them. Father was an aide to the tsar. Claims to be in her sixties. Came here from France where the family fled after the Revolution. Immensely successful. Seen everywhere but won't allow press interviews or photos. Guards her privacy. Guards the privacy of her clients, too. She's painted three presidents and two queens and everyone else who counts."

50

"And they've all bought houses here?"

"You're where they run on the fast track, kid. And Persis . . ."

"Yes?"

"Don't go mucking about for once. Be careful, will you? Just because nobody's Public Enemy Number One doesn't mean they all play nice."

"Don't be silly, Ed. When have I ever mucked about, as you put it?"

"When haven't you? I get this weird feeling every time you call. You're a nice kid, Persis. But sometimes you don't have a whole lot of sense."

"Yes, yes—I understand." I was anxious to end the conversation. I didn't need a lecture from Ed Simms: I got enough of them from Aunt Lydie and Oliver Reynolds, both of whom seemed to think I couldn't walk across the street without deliberately falling under a car. Not that they hadn't—at times—had reason on their side.

"Please, Persis, listen to me." Every word was laden with pained sincerity. "This time call me before you get in trouble?"

I touched my throat. I touched the spot on my arm where the bullet had grazed me. I wanted to assure him, to say that of course I would call him before I got in trouble. But I couldn't. I was already in trouble.

"Thanks ten zillion, Ed," I said.

"Oh—and there's one other thing."

"Yes?"

"In case you think I'm kidding . . . that terrorist consortium . . . the Coalition . . . remember this . . . it has one reason for being, one single purpose: the overthrow of the western governments as we know them, the destabilization of the world as it now exists, the death of the western democracies. Do you understand, Persis?"

"Oh, God," I said. And I hung up.

Eight

After I hung up I thought briefly of going back to The Crossing and just sitting down and quietly thinking things over. But then I remembered that Aunt Lydie was giving a luncheon for an ambassador the next day, and thought better of it. The Crossing would be buzzing with activity. There would be a million workers swarming all over the place. It was definitely neither the time nor the place for sweet contemplation.

I ought to return the van. After all, I had more or less pirated it, swearing poor old Roberts to secrecy as he drove me to the gallery where I stole the keys from Withers's desk and the sacred van more or less from under her nose.

But it was glorious to be on my own for a few hours. I had, I realized, been a virtual prisoner all this time, albeit a pampered one. It was fun to be free.

And the van was full of gas.

I ought to make the most of it.

And I ought to begin with Nadia Milonsky, the indomitable countess. She seemed to be the star of this affair.

I straightened my shoulders and strengthened my resolve, feeling like a knight girding himself for battle, except that my noble steed was an art gallery van. Well, people had gone into battle less well mounted than that.

Nadia Milonsky.

It takes a collection of very special gifts to be the foremost portrait painter in the world, which was currently the

52

position occupied by Nadia Milonsky. There had been many great ones in the past: Velázquez, Goya, Van Dyck, Ingres, Rembrandt, Monet, Renoir, Sargent, Degas, Eakins. To survive, the artists had to be as temperamental, eccentric, tough, and overbearing as their clients. The will of the subject more often than not had to submit to the ego of the painter for there to be a successful outcome. In most cases the artist won. But there had been many occasions in which the sitter and the artist engaged in a monumental clash. These contests often ended in the death of the portrait, as for example, in the case of the famous "lost" portrait of Churchill painted by Graham Sutherland— Churchill could not tolerate the artist's version of him and so the portrait disappeared.

Painters of kings and princes, history has showed, could not be milque-toasts. Madame Milonsky was not a milquetoast.

Still, she always managed her affairs with consummate grace. And no one had ever destroyed one of her portraits.

To begin with, she was, as she frankly admitted, a "society artist," catering to the wealthy and the powerful. The deep psychological aspects of the sitter did not interest her. What she looked for in a subject was the best possible view, presented in the most illustrious and luxurious setting. "I want to do portraits," she once said, "that will make all my sitters . . . even a hundred years from now . . . look like kings and queens." If the client was short, she made him look tall by raising the sitter's chair and painting him from below. If the client was fat, she veiled the body in shadow. If the client was ugly, she found a single attractive feature and dramatized it. No one came away dissatisfied.

Furthermore, there was snob appeal. She was very chic. As a child of the Russian court, she explained casually, she spoke five languages impeccably. Her jewels were the equal of anyone's. She had painted everyone of importance and traveled everywhere in doing it. She was elegant, imperious, and amusing.

She was, in short, a personage. And she was about to paint four people, one of whom might have known Lassiter was in the south of France.

I had to talk with her. I like to do everything right now. Aunt Lydie says it's my fatal weakness. She has a new fatal weakness for me every week. So does Oliver Reynolds.

I had to talk to Nadia Milonsky because in everything you must begin at the beginning, and the beginning had been Lassiter's trip to France. At least, it had been the beginning for me. His being in France had precipitated his assassination, and that had drawn men into his garden. Their presence had, in turn, dragged me into the affair. Now the question was, who knew Lassiter was in France before he was killed?

Someone had told Nadia Milonsky . . . someone who knew. So I had to see her.

But it wasn't, of course, easy. When I called her house an ancient male retainer who could scarcely speak English informed me that she was at Kennedy Airport, about to fly to France. Kennedy Airport is a place to which only a madman would drive himself in mid-day. The traffic is abominable; so is the parking. And there was a time limit.

I strapped myself in, clenched my teeth, said a prayer, and took off like Fred Fearless fired from the cannon. And when I opened my eyes I was there. So was Nadia Milonsky, dominating everything as far as the eye could see.

She was standing near the Air France ticket counter. Her steel gray wig, so lofty and curled and eye-catching that you never noticed her face, was firmly in place. So were her corsets. She dominated the scene with the serene nobility of the Winged Victory of Samothrace dominating the hordes that toil upstairs at the Louvre.

She saw me and her voice soared easily above the mob.

54

"Persis . . . what a magnificent coincidence! You are going to Paris, too?"

Her newest young secretary was at the first-class counter, almost invisible behind a mountain of matched luggage. There had been several young secretaries over the years, all of them handsome and bulging with muscle.

Madame had divorced herself from the boring preflight details and was standing aloofly to one side.

"They're trying to make me pay overweight: they always do," she whispered in a tone designed to shake the rafters. "It's always the same battle. And me, an old lady like me—why do they harass me? And a starving artist at that!" The diamond encrusted gold pin on her shoulder flickered dimly in agreement.

"Your paints and canvases?" I pointed to the luggage.

"No. My clothes, I'm afraid. It's always the same battle—they *will* not understand that I must make a good appearance."

"Your houseman told me you were off to Paris for two weeks . . . I thought perhaps it was a commission."

"My dear Persis—this is not entirely a working expedition. . . . Oh, no. But it's partly work. That child who's married to Hallsey Bryce . . . too young to have any character so the gown must be superb. We'll pick one in Paris. Not that there's any urgency—he won't allow her to be done until I'm through with him—the male ego is astonishing. But it's a good excuse. I'll do the great couture houses by day and a few small dinners by night. It will be such fun. I will arrange to have you invited, too, Persis . . . you're a charming addition to any party. I can't think, as a matter of fact, why I haven't done your portrait."

I could think why: Madame's fees varied between $200,000 and the unthinkable, depending on the client. I couldn't afford either end of the spectrum.

"I'm not going to Paris, Madame."

She wasn't listening. "You really have stunning cheekbones. And I've noticed your eyes—sometimes they're

55

green, sometimes they're gray. Very fascinating.'' She was studying my face with fierce, professional concentration. It was as if a giant spotlight had been turned on me. I squirmed.

"I'm truly flattered. But. . . .''

"I do think, however, that your hair could be improved, if you'll forgive my saying so. It needs civilizing. It needs direction. There's a great new man at Arden's. . . .''

"It might have been the wind in the parking lot. Also, I was running to catch you.''

The spotlight snapped off. "To catch me?''

"Yes. I had to drive like a madman to get here in time.''

The murky dark eyes flickered. "How strange. Why did you do that?''

Her secretary had left the ticket counter and chose this minute to interrupt. "Madame—the money. . . .''

"Gracious, Armand—can't you do anything by yourself?'' Then, turning back to me and speaking in the same ear-shattering whisper, she confided, "It has to do always with money. He's no good at it, I'm afraid. None of them are. But he's very useful in other ways. As an escort, for instance. He barely understands the language, and that's good. Also he's safe, being a *cycliste.*''

"Cyclist? You mean he's a bicyclist?''

"Heavens no, Persis . . . I mean what I say—a *cycliste* . . . something to do with pedals. Isn't that the proper French word? Gay, my dear. Light as a feather and no threat at all sexually. It's perfectly lovely. Now stay right here—you look divine—and I'll settle this and be right back.''

She turned from me and moved with great dignity toward the counter, steaming past the five or six other first-class passengers waiting in line with the insouciance of a mighty steel-topped ocean liner passing a string of dinghies.

There was a brief exchange. It ended with Madame digging in her purse and emerging with a gigantic role of

56

money from which she counted out a collection of bills to lay before the awestruck Air France clerk. In a credit-card world, it was given to few to see such wads of the real thing. The luggage was then piled on the conveyor by the gasping young secretary, who watched with relief as it slowly disappeared.

Madame swam with stately nobility back to me.

"That's that," she said without rancor. She snapped her bag shut with a loud click. "Now why did you come rushing out here to see me? What's it all about?"

I took a big breath. "It's about Sir Courtney Lassiter."

"Lassiter? I don't believe it." Her voice soared. "I *don't* believe it. You, too? Is every woman in Gull Harbor on his trail?"

"No, Madame. I didn't come here to chase Lassiter. I just want to know who told you he was in France?"

"Why come all the way here for that?"

"Something about the house," I mumbled. "Need to be in touch. Thought that person would know. . . ."

"That antiquated Beau Brummell . . . that obsolete roué? Who would care where he is? The equipment, I'm sure, needs an overhaul." She released a peal of laughter that could be heard throughout the terminal. People set down their luggage and stared.

I tried not to look as astonished as I was feeling. Madame and Lassiter? Could they have been partners in some final geriatric fling?

Again the great laugh ricocheted around the waiting room. "Dear girl, I haven't the faintest idea who told me. Can't remember. Unimportant to me. Sorry. I can't concern myself with old fossils turned out to grass by their services. British Intelligence—shipped over here to finish out his days passing back useless scraps of noninformation through the Old Boy network. Silly old goat. Passé. Finished. Who cares where he is?"

"Intelligence? You know that?"

"I don't know, silly girl—just guessing. But why else

57

would Bobby Blessing be sponsoring him? Surely you know that Bobby was a charter member of the OSS when it was all society and the best schools? First they played polo and rowed for their schools, then they all went to war and joined the OSS. My dear, we Russians come from a civilization schooled in such things . . . I can smell it a million miles away.''

A slight exaggeration, surely; yet it made a mad kind of sense. Two old men, still playing cops and robbers.

One of them now dead.

I tried once more. "I was hoping you would remember who told you he was in France. It would be so helpful, Madame.''

She pretended to mop her eyes, as if tears of amusement were spilling out of them. They weren't. "Courtney Lassiter . . . imagine you thinking his whereabouts were so important I'd remember who told me. Child, he's an old has-been. And dull, dull, dull.'' Having disposed of the unfortunate Lassiter, she turned to more interesting things. "I'll see you in a week or so, Persis. I'm coming back for the Artists' and Models' Ball—I must support my own. So must you, being in the trade, as it were. What are you coming as? I'm thinking of Catherine of Russia, the empress, you know. It's a good thing occasionally to remind everyone that there was such a thing as a Russian aristocracy.''

In the recent confusion I'd completely forgotten about the Ball. "I hadn't thought.''

"And there's the cocktail party on Martin's yacht before. Ah, *les nouveaux riches! Quand même, je suis très contente qu'ils soient mes clients. Mon Dieu*—I suppose I shall spend a fortune on myself in the couture houses this week, but I must, after all, be decently turned out for all the summer fêtes, don't you agree?'' A slight film glazed her eyes as she contemplated the festivities to come: it was at such social events that she harvested new clients.

The couture houses were not my territory, so I plunged off on another tack. "Madame, do you ever work from photo-

58

graphs?'' It was just something to say. But I might as well have asked her if she tore the wings from butterflies.

The great curl-crowned head swung on me fiercely. ''Photographs? That's heresy, young woman.''

''I didn't mean to insult you. Forgive me.''

There was a thunderously silent pause. Then she relented. ''Of *course* I work from photographs. How else would I get anything accomplished? Can you imagine the queen of England, for instance, posing for all the hours required to do a decent portrait? Some artists make a plaster cast of their sitters' bodies to save their having to sit. I take photographs.''

''Are you good?''

''Acceptable. I learned in Paris before the war. I know all I need to know for my work.''

I wanted to pursue it. ''I'm a terrible photographer. Who taught you?''

But the secretary was back. ''Time to move upstairs, Madame.''

She did not rebel. ''All right, Armand—I'm coming. My dear Persis, I'm so sorry you're not joining us. Imagine your coming all the way out here to ask about a broken down old rake.''

Armand took her by the elbow and began to shepherd her through the crowds toward the escalator. He was like a small child towing a magnificent remnant of Imperial Russia—a remnant resplendent in a purple velvet suit and a diamond and pearl pin with matching earrings that would have given a jewel thief a heart attack.

Just before they disappeared I thought I heard a trumpet blast. But it was only Madame.

''The Ball,'' she cried: and vanished in the general direction of heaven.

So that was that. Nadia Milonsky, whom I had hoped would provide the answer to one of the two puzzles I had kept from Blessing and Dana, had evaporated before my very eyes, together with any hope I might have of learning who

59

had been aware of Lassiter's trip to the south of France, a trip that Blessing had said no one knew about.

She didn't remember. She was on her way to Paris. And even when she returned, I couldn't go on asking her. She'd said she didn't remember, and from the way she said it, I knew it was final.

What next?

That, at least, was a question I could answer.

Next was the Lydia Wentworth luncheon for the ambassador to Bonn.

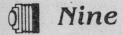 *Nine*

I tend to forget that my aunt, Lydia Wentworth, lives life at a very high and speedy level. I forget because, despite her limousines and her racing stable and her art collection and her houses scattered carelessly here and there around the world, she is quite without airs. It makes one forget.

Her reception for the ambassador to Bonn reminded me.

The Russian–East German–West German–American situation was touch and go. Things were so ticklish, in fact, that the ambassador had been called back to Washington for a Cabinet-level conference. Now he had his instructions and was about to rush back to his post.

But not before he saw Aunt Lydie.

"He's an old beau," she told me, "and he insists on lunching with me before his plane leaves for Bonn. You'll love him—he's handsome." She and I share a *tendresse* for handsome men.

Aunt Lydie's idea of lunching with the ambassador was

60

to invite a zillion Republican millionaires to join them for a "snack" at The Crossing and to organize everything on literally a day's notice. Orders flew this way and that. The broad acres of The Crossing disappeared beneath a carpet of caterers, decorators, florists, tent raisers, car parkers, security people, and waiters. A year's work was accomplished in hours.

"It must be done right," my aunt kept saying. "Philip is the most important man in the world at this minute. One word from him and countries will fall." My aunt is great at exaggeration.

"Is he married?" I asked, feeling a twinge of sympathy for any wife who had to contend with Lydia Wentworth.

She looked pleased. "Oh, no—there was never anyone but me. I didn't want to marry. I still don't. He was sweet about it—he said he'd wait for me forever." The word "forever" appeared to give her pause: she took a deep breath and fixed me with an anxious eye. "Do you think he'll find me still attractive?" She held her breath and waited.

I gave her the right answer because it was true. "He'll find you smashing."

The glamorous, glittery lady relaxed. "I do hope you're right."

She'd put on her new Galanos dress for the occasion, and as if that weren't spectacular enough, she was wearing the famous Wentworth pearls.

"Oh, yes," I assured her, "he'll fall at your feet."

And he did. But not exactly the way I'd meant it.

The luncheon looked like an Impressionist painting come to life.

Aunt Lydie decided that it should be held outdoors. She had consulted the *Farmer's Almanac* and it gave her the go-ahead.

"Sunny and mild, it says. The *Almanac* has never betrayed me." And she gave orders for the gardens to be

61

resodded, the hedges clipped, the intricate brick walks weeded, the five fountains turned on and acres of blooming flowers brought from the greenhouse at the eleventh hour and set in the dirt of the borders in their pots so that they could be whisked back again when the last guest departed.

Her faith in the *Almanac* was almost but not quite boundless—she hedged her bets by contracting for four pink tents to be placed at strategic intervals in case the unthinkable occurred.

"But it won't," she said confidently.

And it didn't. It wouldn't dare.

The day had dawned exactly as planned—the air was soft with spring and the sun shown. A pink canopy, edged by potted rose trees, led from the cobblestone front courtyard to the three acres of gardens. The spring garden was already in bloom, ablaze with daffodils and tulips. The greenhouse gardeners, thirty strong, had created the rest.

Dark green hedges formed intricate patterns in counterpoint to the equally intricate maze of brick walks. White wrought-iron chairs and tables had been artfully scattered throughout, the tablecloths echoing the color of the tents. Every table was graced with moss baskets of white and pink and red flowers. Fresh flowers and tendrils of live ivy climbed up the tent poles.

At the end of the series of gardens—the centerpiece of the whole exquisite picture—was a Chinese folly. It was designed in three soaring arches built of teak in a half circle and embellished with complicated oriental latticework through which the trees in the background formed a green setting. On either side, bas-relief extensions in airy oak patterns concealed wings of brick. The tops of these, screened by potted greenery, formed a terrace reached by winding iron stairs. Seated here was an orchestra. Their orders were not to stray from Cole Porter and they didn't. Below the two wings were a kitchen and a pantry in which the caterers operated like an unseen hive of bees.

In the middle of the large arch, star attraction for the

62

entire view, was a bigger than life-size bronze sculpture of a troop of gypsy acrobats created by one of Aunt Lydie's favorite sculptresses, Rhoda Sherbell. It was a surrealist work, elongated and exaggerated, in which a male acrobat, a masterpiece of ropelike musculature, balanced a girl on his upraised hands. She could have been flying. Two other dancers looked on, poised on their platform like aerialists. They were all almost but not entirely naked, their costumes scanty and rococo, their expressions detached and other-worldly. Lydia Wentworth liked show-stoppers.

She had invited over two hundred guests and they were drifting around the gardens like figures in a dream ballet. The ladies wore large and elaborate hats—hats were the rage this year. From a distance they gave the impression of enormous peonies floating across the green.

Perrier and white wine flowed. An endless series of dishes appeared . . . cold salmons and veals in aspic and vegetables that looked like flower gardens in bloom and soufflés that rose airily and never fell and quiches of every type and dessert crêpes made before one's eyes and cham-pagnes so great that just holding them in a glass was an honor.

Naturally Aunt Lydie and the ambassador were the cata-lysts . . . the action flowed around, but never far from them. He was answering questions, chatting, bowing, smil-ing graciously, but never taking his eyes from my aunt for an instant. She was right—he was handsome.

The scent of money was everywhere, cloying, clinging. There was an ex-king. Afghanistan, I think. There were high-level diplomats. There were senators and governors. There were golf, tennis, and racing greats. Broadway was there. Hollywood, too, with two producers and a clutch of movie stars. There were a couple of oil sheiks. ("I hope they're not planning to buy Gull Harbor," my aunt whis-pered behind their backs.) Oliver Reynolds was there, of course, following me around like a faithful dog. And Nadia Milonsky's four new portrait commissions were there, mingling proudly with her old ones and trying hard to look blasé, as if they were invited to Lydia Wentworth's every day. Martin was rushing around kissing hands and talking too much in his thick French accent; Bryce's uninteresting little wife was doing the same. It was a mistake: in these circles Overspeak spelled Underbred. Never mind, I told myself—they'll learn. The Milonsky portrait is the first step. And Martin has already managed to corner everyone with the party on his yacht. Would Gull Harbor ever discover that his money came from porno films? Probably not. They'd rather be drawn and quartered than admit they'd even heard of one.

Hans von Berger's head was a golden tower surrounded by fluttering lady moths attracted to the golden light. His problem was not Overspeak—he was barely opening his mouth. He inclined his elegant body this way and that, smiling, his beautiful head nodding politely. There was something familiar about him—but what? I decided I was imagining things.

Hallsey Bryce stood against a boxwood hedge, glowering . . . a sinister spider waiting for a bug to fly into his web. But who, I wondered? Was he already bored with his child bride? I watched the arrogance with which he shook off the one or two polite guests who tried to be nice to him. And I wondered.

Looking at them all there together, I couldn't imagine which one might have known about Lassiter. He was a lady's man, according to Nadia Milonsky. Could it have been Bryce's wife? Had she a mysterious past? Had Lassiter known her before she married Bryce? Possible, I supposed. Martin . . . he was French . . . he had a yacht . . . yachts went to the south of France. Was he the one? Von Berger. Very, very possible—an aircraft dealer went everywhere and knew everyone. Yes, very possible. And Bryce, the inventor with no visible inventions. What about him? He looked mean enough to order anyone's assassination. Suppose he'd learned that Lassiter and his wife. . . .

64

But it was all idle speculation. What did I actually know? Nothing.

The party swirled around me and especially around Aunt Lydie and the ambassador. You couldn't see my aunt's silver head because of the crowds surrounding her and her guest. I wasn't doing badly, either. I was wearing a very modest dress but the skirt was slit to alarming heights.

The music was great. A few guests were dancing. I blessed my aunt for having the party outdoors: indoors the noise would have been deafening.

I tried to keep an eye on the four new Milonsky commissions but it was difficult. They had split up after their first greeting and were now lost in the crowd.

I looked around to see who else was present.

Bobby Blessing was there, naturally, looking quite out of sorts, and Dana—Dana was one of the men not following me: in fact, he scarcely looked my way. Cochran was there, but as a guest because she was Gull Harbor, not as the Press: Aunt Lydie never allowed the Press. And at the very last possible instant—Madame Milonsky. She appeared on the terrace with the unexpectedness of a booming thunderclap on a flawless summer day and cried out in a voice guaranteed to reach the last row in any balcony: "My darlings—I hadn't the least idea when Lydia invited me that I'd be able to get back from Paris for this occasion; but *there* was Laurence at dinner last night and when he heard my problem he lent me his private jet so I could be here to greet my beloved Philip, whom I haven't seen since the portrait in Bonn five years ago. And that heavenly man— the plane is waiting to take me back!"

It was so well done that there was a burst of applause and a rush forward to greet her as if she, and not the ambassador, were the true star of the occasion.

"Sporting old girl," said the ambassador.

"Scene stealer," said my aunt, who was an expert one herself.

"Champagne, champagne," said Nadia Milonsky and every one had champagne and toasted her.

65

It was in the middle of this that Aunt Lydie gave me the signal that the ambassador was about to depart. "He'll just creep away, Persis . . . he doesn't want to break up the party. Keep an eye on things for me while I slip out to the car to say good-bye. I'll be right back."

They moved away casually. They paused behind an enormous Chinese vase filled with spring flowers. Then they disappeared.

I did as I'd been told, drifting from group to group, chatting with everyone and trying to be Aunt Lydie. Chatting wasn't easy: even outdoors the noise level was astonishing.

Still I heard it. Or maybe I sensed it—it could have been that. Nor was I alone: it was the waiters—they stopped whatever they were doing and, for the briefest of seconds, were still and listening. Then they were moving—fast. They were running. I ran too. Because I knew about the waiters. They were Security.

The tableau vivant was arranged in the courtyard, at the very steps of Lydia Wentworth's house.

Except that it was really a tableau mort.

She was there, standing on the next-to-the-bottom step like a waxwork image. The ambassador lay at her feet, his gray hair very red, the unreal red of a Halloween wig that had been dyed, even so, a more bizarre than usual color.

There were men crouched in firing position. There were bodies. There was a strange, burned smell to the air.

It was a frozen second during which no one moved, as if afraid to spoil a perfect composition.

Then there was an explosion of action. Shouts. Men running. Walkie-talkies crackling. Sirens in the distance. Men bending over the ambassador at Aunt Lydie's feet.

She alone had not moved. I could tell from her waxen look that she was in shock.

"The kind of attack you can't stop," someone said.

"They infiltrated the drivers," said another voice. "The chauffeurs."

"Aunt Lydie—please. . . ." I put my arm around her. She was in a trance. "I never saw it happen."

"Please—let's go in. They're doing everything they can for him."

"He's dead." I could barely hear her.

"Oh, Aunt Lydie. . . ."

"He promised to wait forever. And forever came."

She turned and walked into the house. Her back was very straight. But I knew she was crying. Blessing was at her side. So was I.

"Take care of her," he ordered, as she stepped inside. He stared at the devastation behind us.

"It has begun," he said.

Ten

There was no thought now of my going home. Aunt Lydie needed me. She wouldn't need me long: she would stop grieving in a week or so and after that it would be as if the ambassador had never existed. It was her way of dealing with catastrophes. But for the moment she needed me.

So I stayed—through police and detectives and reporters and press photographers and, almost as bad, through endless friends who called night and day to inquire after Aunt Lydie's health and to learn what inside facts they could about the shooting.

Mercifully the ambassador's funeral was held quietly at Arlington and my aunt was too "ill" to go, so we were spared that.

67

"It can't help now . . . it's all over for him. So why put ourselves through it?" And she didn't budge from her bed.

Not once did she ask who was responsible for the assassination: it had happened, and the "why" of it didn't interest her. But it interested me. The trouble was I couldn't find out anything about it. No one took credit for the attack. Ed Simms was not answering my phone calls and Blessing and Dana were elusively nonpresent. I tried to reach them several times. I had decided to tell them the little I knew that they did not know. The ambassador's assassination had convinced me that it was time. But they seemed to have disappeared and nobody was about to say where. There wasn't anyone else I dared talk to. I would have to wait for their reappearance.

The press remained occupied with the Ambassador to Bonn Affair, as they called it, for several days. Having no hard information, they trotted out all their favorite terms and flung them about at random like an overage baseball pitcher hurling balls toward home plate in the fond hope that one would turn out to be a strike. "Terrorists," "trained assassins," "international plot," and "upsetting the balance of power" were terms that surfaced often.

But after a period during which no real information made itself available, they lost interest and abandoned the hunt.

The minute they did Lydia Wentworth revived.

"I think I'll go to Paris in a week or so." She was leafing through the *Times* and drinking her morning coffee, both with more energy than she'd displayed in days.

"Really?" I was surprised. It was a sudden recovery, even for her.

"I must look after my health. Nobody loves a sick woman."

I noted with some amazement that she was looking quite splendid again. "That's true."

Did I sound sardonic? I may have, because she plunged her nose deep into her newspaper and didn't look at me.

"This Dutch kidnapping," she continued after a long pause, " . . . they'll never bother with me. I have let it be

68

known to my men of affairs that not one cent is to be paid if I'm kidnapped."

Her color had come back and her eyes were sparkling. She was definitely on the mend. I'd had no time for anything but her since the ambassador's death: now, maybe, I could get my act back together. Lassiter . . . Praha . . . there was so much to think about. And I had to find Blessing and Dana: I had to tell them.

She was still talking. "Not one single solitary cent of tribute is to be paid on my behalf if I am ever 'snatched'— I believe that's the word?" She loves to be up to date. "And I've let it be known everywhere. So that's that. If anyone's sniffing around with an eye to putting the snatch on me, they'll soon give it up."

No one who really knew Lydia Wentworth could imagine that she'd pay one penny of ransom: even bankers were not as hard to separate from their money as she.

She rattled the newspaper for emphasis, then continued. "It's so interesting—the president is going to France in two months. It's for a Super Summit of all the Western heads of state to see if they can't douse the flames of the Bonn-Kremlin situation. If conflict breaks out—and Russian tanks are already poised on the West German frontier—all of western Europe will be involved. That's what it says here. Of course, it's nonsense. Jiggs says he will straighten it all out and the flap will die without a whimper."

I knew what Jiggs she was talking about—she meant the president of the United States. They were long-time friends: Lydia Wentworth's support had a lot to do with his being in office.

I wasn't as optimistic as she. "Perhaps . . . but there's always the Near East business."

"Tempest in a hookah." She laughed, very pleased with herself. I refrained from mentioning that a hookah and a teapot do not serve the same purpose: a hookah is for smoking, of which Aunt Lydie does not approve.

She poured some hot water into her coffee from the sil-

69

ver Guernsey jug on her tray. "I talked to Marianne and Jiggs this morning. They'll dine with me in Paris so I must go over in advance—the house needs looking after." A wild exaggeration if ever I heard one. Her Paris staff was so excellent that even the Rothschilds had tried to seduce them away from her.

But I didn't demur. "Of course you must, Aunt Lydie."

"Marianne says she's going mad trying to choose her wardrobe for the trip. She doesn't know if they'll travel by plane or barrage balloon. The Secret Service is so hysterical after the attack on Philip that nobody knows the plans."

"One can't blame them."

"I'll go shortly after the Artists' and Models' Ball. It's a cause we must all support—those starving artists. What are you wearing? It's in the bowels of New York City, you know."

People in Gull Harbor will go to the ends of the earth to dance around in fancy dress. I don't understand it; but that's the way it is.

I had forgotten again. "I haven't thought of anything."

"You must. My dear, you've been wool-gathering for days. You promised."

A small flicker of excitement stirred within me. Dana was certain to be a wonderful dancer—I could tell by the way he moved. I would think of something wildly seductive and clinging—I do have a good figure. We would dance the night away.

But Bobby Blessing resurfaced to break the news, by phone, that Dana would not be back. "He's gone. Called back to Washington."

"Did he leave a message for me?"

"None. He's a busy man, Persis."

I combed the newspapers for a clue. I don't know why. Perhaps it was some dim idea that his disappearance would have a link to current events. But nothing seemed pertinent: the press was single-mindedly preoccupied with the fact that the French had developed a successor to Exocet which

70

could search and destroy both surface and sub-surface craft. From all the uproar it was obviously a happening of some import, but not to me. All I was interested in was Alexander Dana. Wherever he was, it would have something to do with Lassiter. That was the only thing I considered a certainty.

My good spirits departed as suddenly as a houseguest when the weather turns bad.

The single note of cheer was a call from Kate Cochran.

"Persis? Try Marcel Martin."

I wasn't tracking. "For what?"

"For what you want to know."

"About . . . ?"

"About the photographer, Praha. I've just been at Martin's house doing an interview about international cruising and I've learned from the host himself that he's the proud owner of one of the world's most complete libraries of pornographic literature. He considers it a collection of great art."

"Did you see . . . ?"

"He showed me everything. A big paneled room *full.* Wow! Even I did some blushing. But no Praha."

My heart sank. "Oh."

"So I asked him . . . how come you don't have this famous book by Praha? It's one of the most famous unseen books in the world. Every great collection should have it. And you know what he said?"

Now my heart began beating again, very fast. "What?"

"He said, I do. Probably the only copy left. But I don't keep it here. Sorry I can't show it to you. The implication was that it was in a bank vault somewhere, right?"

"Right."

"But you know collectors, Persis—you know them better than I do. They like to look at their treasures, not lock them away. So . . . want to bet it's somewhere where he can lay his hands on it whenever he wants? After all, it has to be the star of his collection."

71

"Somewhere near. Like. . . ."

"That's it . . . like his yacht. The last place anyone would think he'd keep something that valuable. And I'll never be invited there. I'm not chic enough, but you are. I know that you're all going there before the Ball."

"You're right, Cochran. If I find it, I promise I'll tell you about it the minute I do."

"You'll find it, Persis. Call me instantly. I'm betting on you."

I was glad she was so confident.

〚﹆〛 *Eleven*

A string of gleaming limousines and bright taxis wound like a sinuous black and gold serpent through the grubby streets of Hell's Kitchen on New York's west side. Ordinarily, Hell's Kitchen is not a neighborhood knowledgeable New Yorkers frequent after dark: but tonight it was transformed, at least on the route to the KIKI Klub, which was hosting the Artists' and Models' Ball. The streets had been stripped of their garbage—the sidewalks swept of their drunks. No one was being mugged.

All this had happened by order of the mayor himself because a collection of famous art patrons was venturing out of its platinum-lined lairs to mingle with the Bohemian inhabitants of New York's famous lofts.

I was driving in style in my aunt's aged limousine with its Lalique bud vases, its ample running boards, and its venerable chauffeur, Roberts, at the wheel. Sharing the er-

72

mine lap robe with me was Lydia Wentworth and perched uncomfortably on the jump seat was Bobby Blessing.

We were creeping along patiently behind an enormous hired limo which in turn was following a long line of assorted expensive vehicles from which an occasional masked head emerged to demand why we were progressing so slowly. The costumes dimly visible inside the cars gave the whole procession a vaguely Alice-in-Wonderland look.

The trip in on Martin's yacht had been in itself a Wonderlandlike experience. We had boarded the *Greater Gatsby* at Seawanhaka Corinthian Yacht Club, helped aboard by uniformed stewards. Drinks had begun to flow immediately, as barmen struggled to keep their balance once we were under way, and maids teetered about the deck with hors d'oeuvres and stumbled up and down the steps to the galley below.

I was definitely not the smash hit of the evening, costume-wise, as they say in New York. By the time I finally realized that there was no way—absolutely none—that I was going to escape this soirée, the Gull Harbor locusts had denuded the costumers and there was nothing left but a third act curtain *Chorus Line* dress. Well, not exactly a dress—but tailcoat, top hat, mesh stockings, and cane, all in gold.

The plot was to have our cars meet us at the South Street Seaport to transport us to the Ball. I was cadging a ride with Aunt Lydie: at a party like this it's nice to go first class all the way.

There were probably a hundred and fifty guests on the yacht. Floating down Long Island Sound with a hundred and fifty characters in fancy dress is not an everyday experience. Even Aunt Lydie was startled. I'm not sure who Aunt Lydie herself was supposed to be and I didn't dare ask; but she was done up in yards and yards of pink tulle and pink feathers and pink-dyed pearls. The moment we boarded the *Gatsby* she looked around and peered wonderingly through her pink silk and pearl-encrusted mask.

73

"Persis," she demanded, "who *are* these people? I'm sure that I don't know any of them!" As she spoke a cloud of pink feathers separated themselves from her headdress and floated down around her, creating a rather celestial effect.

"Well, you certainly recognize me," said a Kodiak bear.

"Oh, *you*, Bobby. Of course. But you kept warning me."

I looked around with a sort of bedazzled interest. The scene was already quite bizarre. What would it be like, I asked myself, after a drink or two?

"That big Cossack has to be Nadia Milonsky," the Kodiak bear announced.

"I thought she was going to be Catherine the Great of Russia?" She'd practically promised.

"She found just in time that Sonny Thrasher's wife was coming as Catherine, though heaven knows she's not Russian . . . actually, she's from Mobile, I believe." My aunt snorted a little—she was not mad about Mobile. Too hot.

"The mayor of New York is here as a Mets' ballplayer."

"And the governor's a Yankee . . . he always was a money man." Aunt Lydie wasn't being critical, just pragmatic. "But the mayor's always been for the underdog."

I looked around for Hallsey Bryce and his wife and for Von Berger and our host. I never did find Bryce but he must have been there because his wife, sweet and demure as Little Bo Peep, was sipping champagne from the same glass as a big, handsome Musketeer I recognized as Ronald Chunk, the real estate tycoon. So much, Bryce, for marrying a child.

I spotted Hans von Berger in the milling crowd. He was not hard to find because he was dressed as the compleat World War I German flyer, complete with goggles and white scarf. He cut quite a dashing figure and I heard him telling people he was wearing the actual flying costume of the famous ace, Von Richthofen. "I collect flight memorabilia," he said to the crowd of admiring women clustered

74

around him. It is absolutely necessary in Gull Harbor to collect *some*thing.

"Ah," they all cried, wigs and masks and hoop skirts bobbing, "How romantic!" They would probably have said the same thing no matter what he was collecting. Once again I found him familiar; once again I was baffled as to why.

The yacht gave a sudden lurch just then and a Marie Antoinette fell down the stairs into the main saloon, where she remained in a stately heap until champagne was brought and she was assured that nothing had been broken. Whereupon she rose and rejoined the revelry.

"That woman is from Connecticut. Greenwich, to be exact." The way Bobby Blessing said it you would have thought Greenwich was Outer Siberia. "What would you expect?"

Just then I spotted Martin. He cut a rather startling figure as Nijinsky in *L'Après-Midi d'un Faun*. He was, in fact, wearing next to nothing. I wondered if he wouldn't freeze before the night was over. Then I saw that he was dragging a goatskin robe behind him.

"She's just under one hundred feet long," I heard him explaining to the little group of oddities that surrounded him. "Ninety feet, three inches, to be exact. That's so she can go through the Panama Canal without paying the fee on ships of one hundred feet and up."

It seemed a good enough reason to me.

"Where was she built?" someone demanded.

But I never heard the answer because Young Abe Lincoln (Oliver Reynolds, actually) had appeared on my port side. "Persis . . . don't forget, you're saving the first three dances for me. You gave your word."

"Did I?"

He looked disapprovingly at my gold sequined mask and mesh clad legs. "Maybe it should be four."

"Don't forget me." It was Gregor Olitsky, my employer. He had come as the Eiffel Tower, a rig so imprac-

75

tical that I was sure he would never get off the yacht, let alone onto the dance floor. One of his sculptors had made it for him—I'd been hearing rumors off and on for months. It was an exact ten-foot replica of the *Tour Eiffel* with Gregor hidden inside the aluminum central cone. Oliver took one look at this ungainly apparition and drifted discreetly off to starboard.

"Damn it, Persis, how am I going to dance in this thing?" Gregor is a marvelous dancer and ladies will stop at nothing to get into his arms on the dance floor.

"I think you'll have to take it off."

He did not want practical advice. "But damn it, Persis, I had it specially built! You're clever—what can I do?"

I knew my employer: he would make a dramatic entrance at the Ball if it killed him. "If I were you, I'd hire two or three of the *Gatsby*'s crew to go with you and prop you up," I advised. "I can't understand how you ever got up the gangplank in that thing in the first place."

"I didn't. I dressed here."

"In Martin's stateroom? Which way is it?"

Gregor gave directions. I started off.

Pathetic little bleats of anguish followed me. "Persis—don't desert me . . . I can't move and I need champagne."

"I'll send some." I kept going. If I didn't find the book soon it would be too late. We'd be at the dock before I knew it.

The stateroom was more like a presidential suite than an ocean-going bedroom. The paneling was walnut, the furniture was William and Mary, the paintings were original Gainsboroughs, and the carpeting was oriental. Next to the enormous bed was a bookcase with a dozen or so volumes. I wasted no time but sat carefully on the satin bedspread and began to check them out. *Parisian Nights* was number six, right in plain sight, just like *The Purloined Letter*.

I went through it once, swiftly. I went through it again, slowly.

Then I heard footsteps. They were brisk, authoritative.

76

And they were headed my way. I dove into the adjacent dressing room. It had a long counter with a long mirror above it. By standing behind the door and leaving it ajar I commanded a perfect view of bookcase and bed.

A massive Cossack marched into the room. Without an instant's hesitation, the figure moved to the bookcase and began to examine the books. When the correct one turned up, the Cossack undid his tunic and stuffed the volume inside. Then the Cossack turned and quick-marched out of the stateroom and through the saloon.

I left the stateroom and dashed up the companionway. We would soon be docking in Manhattan. I must not let Nadia Milonsky out of my sight. More specifically, I must not let *Parisian Nights* out of my sight.

Twelve

The entrance of the KIKI Klub was bedlam. TV camera crews jostled the arriving guests. Microphones were thrust into masked faces. Guests struggling to press inside were further frustrated by ticket takers demanding credentials.

The large number of exotic masks didn't help matters. Some stood out a foot or more from the wearer's head and contributed to the disorder.

Aunt Lydie and Bobby disappeared. I don't know how we got separated but they must have been recognized as VIPs and whisked inside while I was still trapped behind someone wearing a giant lampshade.

The logjam broke unexpectedly; and everyone was swept inside with the swiftness of rushing flood waters.

77

I don't know what I had expected . . . a long winding staircase, perhaps, down which sultry models would glide like goddesses. Gentlemen adoring them. Flowers. Violins.

This was something else—more, I suppose, like the original Balls of the twenties and thirties. There were some painted naked bodies. There was the heavy smell of pot. There were affluent types pausing to sniff cocaine.

The lighting was early Stygian. Body pressed to body in uninvited intimacy. Somewhere in the infernal gloom rock music howled and pounded. The human stream flowed slowly and relentlessly in that direction: I was carried along.

On a balcony to our left there was more TV. I saw the "7" on a camera. I saw Roger Grimsby, the anchorman, bathed in brilliant artificial light and looking every inch as celebrated as the celebrities he was there to interview. A murmur of "Grimsby, Grimsby," swept through the crowd as we oozed past and he smiled down at us, like a pope.

"And there's Ginevra, this year's top model," someone shouted ecstatically, as if he had just been permitted a vision.

"Oh . . . ahhhhh," we all moaned.

"And there's Luciana Marino in red, the TV personality." I loved the way the populace identified everyone we ought to be impressed by.

"Ahhhhh . . . oh."

There she was indeed, standing right next to Grimsby and looking spectacular with her black hair pulled back into a heavy pigtail and her body swathed in a bullfighter's brocade cape. I looked for Oliver, but I didn't see him. Nor did I see Aunt Lydie or Nadia Milonsky.

We squeezed into a new room, leaving the balcony behind. It must have had a bar because people began passing plastic glasses back like a bucket brigade at a number one disaster. A spirit of almost unbridled friendliness now took possession of everyone.

78

"Ever been to a gig like this before?" a Miss Piggy mask demanded of me.

I shook my head and pulled my sequined mask across my face. I thought it would make me seem unfriendly. I thought it would discourage Miss Piggy.

A flash went off—we were too jammed together even to jump. Someone was photographing a model who was backed into a niche in the wall. She was wrapped in transparent gauze. I was glad Oliver wasn't with me—he would have been scandalized. Oliver is a Puritan.

My mask was beginning to make me feel claustrophobic. A woman up ahead was apparently in the same predicament. She was done up as a perfume flask with NORELL printed in large letters across her back.

"This place is a firetrap," she cried. "I'm leaving!" But she didn't.

She was correct, of course—it was a firetrap. But how to get out?

"Drink?" A glass of wine arrived, passed by unseen hands. It tasted rather foul. I wondered why, for the price everyone had paid to attend this affair, a passable wine couldn't be served to relieve the agony.

I still couldn't see Oliver. Would he ever be able to find me? It was insufferably hot. Retreat was out of the question. And where on earth were Lydia, Nadia, and Blessing?

I tried to save my sanity by transporting the scene to Paris and imagining myself being carried into a ballroom by the Japanese artist Foujita, as I'd read about it in the past. I would be sitting in a large golden birdcage—and probably naked.

It didn't work: I couldn't imagine it. I was at the wrong ball in the wrong city and I wasn't with Foujita . . . I seemed to be with Miss Piggy. The best I could hope for was simply to drift along and assume Oliver would find me wherever I finally came to rest.

Where I finally came to rest was the Disco Room, a particularly black Hades rent by blinding flashes of light that increased the disorientation already made unbearable by the deafening noise.

"Isn't it great?" someone screamed. "That's the Special Effects Committee."

"Baby, baby . . . show me some stuff," moaned Miss Piggy, still with me through our agonizing journey. "Dance?"

There didn't seem to be any choice. I downed the last gulp from my plastic glass and tossed it into the air, striving to get into the spirit of things.

"Baby, baby, light my fire." Miss Piggy was getting ecstatic.

I wasn't keen on lighting Miss Piggy's fire, but I tried to be polite and I let my hips move to the music.

A new body appeared next to mine, this one wearing a white plaster mask surrounded by a halo of aluminum discs from which dangled other plaster masks in miniature. For an instant I thought it might be Oliver because the new body was so tall. Then I remembered that he was Young Abe Lincoln tonight. I decided that I was having a delusion—my head felt queer. That *terrific* wine, I thought.

Bam . . . bam . . . bam went the music.

I reached toward White Mask to steady myself. "Excuse me. My knees feel funny." It wasn't just my knees . . . everything felt funny.

White Mask wasn't sure he'd heard correctly. "Did you say you feel *sick?*" he shouted.

"No—funny." All I wanted was air. I had to get out . . . breathe . . . walk around. I must not make a fool of myself in this crowd.

White Mask was helping me. So was Miss Piggy. Between them they were clearing a path. "Sick . . . sick," they were saying and people were moving aside.

I tried to hold my head up, but it kept drooping to my chest. My eyes closed. I was losing touch. I could hear remarks as we passed, but they sounded very far away.

"Drunk, poor thing."

"No wonder."

"No. On something, probably."

"Don't be sick on me, if you don't mind."

It was humiliating.

I caught a glimpse of a Guardian Angel beret. Helping, of course. "Make way, make way."

"Back door, please," one of my rescuers said. I was grateful: imagine if the TV cameras at the front door had caught me leaving the Ball in that condition—whatever that condition was.

We changed direction, sliding through a side door and into an adjacent building, stumbling through the dark toward a gleam of light in the back. I could barely see. I could not walk at all.

We were outdoors and they were helping me into a car. I no longer felt sick—just tired. I remember thinking how wonderful it was that there happened to be a car waiting.

Doors slammed. The engine started; and we eased softly into motion.

"Don't be scared." I felt my sleeve being pulled up. I wasn't frightened; and I didn't resist. I couldn't have resisted—I was drowning in inertia.

"This will make you feel better." I felt a prick.

Then nothing.

Nothing at all.

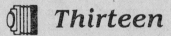 *Thirteen*

I love dreaming. Maybe it's because my dreams are invariably pleasant. I am inclined to dream about beautiful

81

landscapes or wonderful food or dancing with somebody fascinating in front of the Acropolis on a moon-drenched night.

Aunt Lydie, on the few occasions when we have discussed the phenomena, has always maintained that pleasant dreams are the result of a pure conscience.

"I, myself," she proclaims, "have never had a nightmare. Neither have I ever done anything of which I am thoroughly ashamed."

Few mortals, including yours truly, can match this claim. But then, Lydia Wentworth is not an ordinary mortal.

Nonetheless, for whatever reason, my dreams are usually delightful and I've often wished I could have more of them. Like the one in which Craig Claiborne and Pierre Franey teach me to cook. Or the one in which my simple little watercolor is bought by the Metropolitan Museum of Art. I'm also fond of the one in which I kiss a frog and turn immediately into a beautiful princess, although I realize that the real story doesn't end quite like that.

This dream started out pleasantly enough. Mostly it was about Marcel Martin. He was wrapped in his goatskin and we were whirling around the deck of *The Greater Gatsby* in one another's arms. I was cold, and he offered gallantly to include me in his fur wrap but I declined: it might interfere with our dancing and I didn't want that.

The orchestra was sitting in the rigging wearing fantastic animal masks and they were playing something with an insistent Africanlike beat. Martin and I were dancing to it perfectly at first and everybody was applauding, some of them even daring to tap me on the cheeks and shoulders as I whirled by to be certain that I noticed their applause. Everyone was there. I recognized them all on the sidelines. I couldn't make out what they were wearing and they were a little blurred, like scenery seen from le Train à Grande Vitesse, which is the fastest train in the world. But they were there, all right. All of them.

As I said, in the beginning Martin and I were dancing

82

perfectly and everyone approved. Our feet never missed the beat and I floated in his arms as perfectly as if we had been born to dance together. He was smiling at me, his eyes level with mine because he wasn't very tall. "You're wonderful, Persis . . . a wonderful partner. I will dance with you forever."

How nice he is, I thought, floating lightly in his arms. We will go on like this forever while they all applaud.

But gradually the beat changed. We began to stumble. Was it the music? Were we, perhaps, growing tired?

The beat was heavier now—more demanding. It was harder to follow, although louder. What were we supposed to be doing? The tango? The rumba? The merengue? What?

The audience was no longer applauding: they were shouting at us now. "No . . . no. Wrong . . . wrong. You must do better . . . better."

I was freezing. Martin wrapped me inside his goatskin robe and although my body was next to his it didn't help the cold.

"Better! Better! You must do better!"

We stumbled and fell. And when I was finally back on my feet Martin was gone. Bryce was there. But was he? I couldn't tell because of his mask. Von Berger? But no. Where was the golden hair? Nathalie Bryce? What did she really look like, anyway? I had forgotten. She was forgettable. Who were these people and why had they come to the ball if they didn't want to dance? Couldn't they ask the orchestra to play something civilized—something without that mind-altering beat?

But the orchestra wouldn't listen, wouldn't change. So I ran away. I pushed my way through them all, remembering to be polite because I didn't want to offend anyone. "Excuse me, please . . . excuse me. I'm so very sorry but I can't talk to you just now. I must leave, you see."

And somehow I did leave. I don't remember how I got off the yacht—that part is blurred like the faces. But I was on the dock, running. I was running toward a building.

83

And as I approached, it exploded. Flames were everywhere . . . flames in oranges and tomato reds like one of Aunt Lydie's favorite dresses. How beautiful, I thought. Which didn't make sense, because how could a burning building be beautiful?

I should have been afraid. I knew it. I mean, suppose someone was still inside?

But there didn't seem to be any question of that. Whatever was inside was already destroyed. I knew that, too. There was nothing, nothing to be done. Except to admire the beauty of the fiery glow against the black night.

So I just stood and watched. I think I must have been crying at the same time because I heard myself saying "No . . . no . . . no . . . no." But I didn't know why.

Then I saw the figure. He was hunched over and he was running, running, running for his life. He ran in the shadows along the walls of the buildings that lined the street—old buildings and the street scarcely wide enough for a car to pass. I knew he was running for his life and I wanted to run with him, to help.

"Wait—wait . . . I'll come with you."

But I couldn't keep up. He was too far ahead. And anyway, I was freezing—and damp, now, too.

And someone was calling my name.

Someone was wrapping me in warmth.

And calling gently, softly.

"Persis. Persis." Pleading. "Persis. Please."

84

Fourteen

It was like seeing the same movie twice. The cast was the same: the dialogue familiar. Once again the form that was bending over me made me suspect that I had died and gone to heaven.

"Her eyes are open. Persis?" It was Dana.

Bobby Blessing's voice came from somewhere. It had the usual faintly scolding tone, the subtle but unmistakable inference that whatever I'd done should *not* have been done, or done better. "Surely, Persis, you must remember something. All this nonsense about Miss Piggy. How about some practical information? Be a little helpful, please."

"Her color's better. She'll be all right." Dana was plumping up the pillows behind my head and smoothing back my hair. His hand felt cool. "Poor Persis . . . you've been having a hard time, haven't you?"

I wasn't sure, for an instant, that we weren't back at Lassiter's. Then I recognized the French bergères, the escritoire. I was in my room at Aunt Lydie's.

"Alex?"

"Try to make sense, Persis. All you talk about is Miss Piggy and somebody called White Mask." Blessing again.

"Alex—what happened?" I was half sitting up now.

"You're at The Crossing. We had you brought straight here. You're all right. Don't worry." His eyes were so close to me that I had an impulse to step into them and drown in their endless blue.

Bobby sounded furious with me. "You gave us the slip

85

before we got in the front door at the ball and the next thing we knew some fellow walking his dog at three A.M. on the beach found you lying in the wash, overdosed on drugs. Luckily it was just before the tide came in or it would have been bye-bye Persis Willum. We've had them drying you out ever since. It's cost your aunt a fortune, turning this room into a hospital complete with medics and nurses, but she didn't want any publicity.''

"I'm sorry." The ball—had I given them the slip? I tried to remember. It seemed far away and unreal.

Dana still had his hand on my forehead. "She didn't give us the slip; she was deliberately separated from us. They wanted us to think she'd met someone and gone off for a weekend . . . that ambiguous phone message to the house . . . she'd be found later overdosed and drowned. Everyone would assume it was all about drugs.''

"So we had to set up what amounted to a private clinic here because we couldn't take a chance on the hospital reporting . . .''

I felt tears in my eyes.

Dana saw them. "Don't listen to him, Persis. He's upset because we were scared: we thought we'd lost you. And now you must tell us everything you remember because it will help us find whoever did it.''

I tried, for his sake. "I was at the ball. It was crowded. Hot. We got separated—there was someone in a lamp-shade. You were all gone. The wine was terrible. I be-gan to feel queasy—ill. They helped me out, Miss Piggy and . . .''

"White Mask. Yes, we know. What else?''

"A car waiting. I fell asleep. I think I slept a long time. Then questions—always questions I couldn't answer. They were cross.''

"Who, Persis? Who was cross?''

"I don't know.''

"Try to remember.''

86

But it was absurd. They'd never believe me. "Cocteau. Beauty and the Beast. A lion. A frog. A bird."

"Masks," said Dana.

"What did they ask? Remember, Persis—think."

I tried. I really tried. "Well—like a song."

It was the last thing they expected. "A song?"

"Over and over. A refrain. Over and over."

Blessing spoke to Dana as if I weren't present. "The drugs made it seem like that. They were hammering away at one theme."

"Theme—yes, that's it. It was a theme. Like iambs. Like the Morse Code. *Las*-it-ter . . . *Las*-it-ter . . . *Las*-it-ter." It didn't seem like a name to me any more, just a series of notes fiercely accented.

"That's it." They were speaking to each other again and they seemed relieved. "Wanted to know whom she saw in the garden . . . if she could identify . . . wanted to know if she was there on purpose . . . what she knew about Lassiter . . . how big a threat she posed . . . not kidnapping—knew Lydia wouldn't pay . . ."

"All I wanted to do was sleep," I told them.

They didn't listen. "Luckily she didn't know much; but they still tried to kill her . . . and they're on Lassiter's trail . . . moving fast . . . we'll have to move faster."

"Sleep," I said insistently. "I just wanted to sleep."

This time they heard.

"Of course you wanted to sleep . . . that was part of the drug psychology—answer our questions and you can sleep. But now—you're not sleepy now?"

"A little. Not much."

"To be expected. She's still not detoxified." The way he said it, Blessing managed to make it sound faintly immoral. I didn't know what he meant, but it certainly hadn't the cachet of being debriefed, for example. It was more like being defleaed. It was undignified. Unworthy.

I made a great effort, turning to Dana. "If you will please help me sit up a little straighter?" I made my eyes as big

87

as possible to show that I was completely and splendidly de-everything-ed and I stared at Blessing. "If you would be kind enough to order some tea?"

Dana did and Blessing did. And when the tea arrived (it was English Breakfast so I assumed it must be morning), I called up Aunt Lydie's most queenly tone. "And now, gentlemen, you will explain what this is all about."

"You're not well enough. Later, when you're stronger, Persis."

"*Now*," I said. "*Right now.*"

And they knew I meant it.

Fifteen

"If you're sure . . . ." Dana began. "This isn't easy stuff, you know."

"I'm sure."

"Let me." Blessing took over—habit of command, I suppose. He pulled out a gold-tipped black cigarette and made a ceremony of lighting it. "Care for one, Persis?"

I couldn't imagine anything I would care for less at the moment. "No, thank you."

"Damned good. Sobranie . . . made from a blend once reserved for a grand duke at the court of St. Petersburg, so they say.

"Oh."

"You don't mind? Good. Well, then, let's begin."

"I would like that, please. I have been through a lot. I should like to know why."

"Of course. You've earned the right." Blessing blew a

88

long, lean cloud of smoke. "It has to do with money— more than half a billion dollars, to be specific."

"Depending on the rate of exchange, over 500 million dollars today," Dana put in.

"And there are two groups after it—two groups who have been after it for more than forty years: the British and the Russians."

"Three now," Dana added. "We've joined the hunt."

"Russians?" My hands had turned unaccountably cold. I slipped them under the down comforter to warm them.

"No proof, of course. But it began with Czechoslovakia, now part of the Eastern Bloc. It began with Czechoslovakian gold."

Blessing paused to pour a second cup of tea. He had called for a carafe of rum and he poured a judicious two fingers of it into his teacup.

"It was the beginning of World War II—the Czech government was falling: it had already been dismembered by the Munich Pact. Before he resigned, the president of Czechoslovakia, Eduard Benes, made plans to rescue his country's gold—fifty million dollars worth of gold bars— one thousand tons of gold then worth thirty-five dollars an ounce, today worth $373 an ounce. The English agreed to help and to hold the gold in trust until the restoration of Czech independence—a day that never arrived.

"The gold was removed in small quantities and melted down. It was possible to do this because the central Czech bank normally shifted gold from branch to branch over a period of thirty days and thus no suspicion was aroused.

"The melted gold was then poured into dozens of different molds which were painted with opaque paints and packed in rust inhibitors for shipping. The Czechs were great merchants; these molds for replacement parts—for polished steel gears, connecting rods—were typical of their shipping activities. False papers were supplied: the material crossed the border one shipment at a time and rendezvoused in France. It was then up to the British to get it out."

"They did?"

Blessing ignored the interruption. He was not to be rushed. "The British named the operation Boomerang, for the obvious reason that the material was to return eventually to its source. A team of British Intelligence officers was in charge. The French Resistance and a few Czech patriots supplied the manpower. The plan was divided into separate phases, with a different British officer in charge of each—for security reasons. Unfortunately the planned points of exit were shut one by one by the Germans, the swiftness of whose victories surprised everybody. The gold moved from point to point, like a chess game."

"Three years," Dana said under his breath. "Three years of failure."

"And forty years of failure since," Blessing muttered angrily.

It had all happened so long ago; it scarcely seemed germane. "It's a fascinating story. But what does it have to do. . . ."

"Patience. It has everything to do with you—with us." Dana put his finger to his lips to suggest my silence.

Blessing continued, oblivious. "The final desperate plan was to transfer the material to a British cruiser that would rendezvous near Marseille. The convoy snaked its way across Europe to the south of France."

I tried to imagine what it must have been like—this fortune in gold trapped inside an occupied country with no way to get it out. Germans everywhere. The bombing raids. The war.

But I couldn't. It had no reality. It was only pictures in a book—images on a screen. I am an artist. My life is visual. And I couldn't add the final reality that comes to an artist from being present and seeing with his own eyes. It was so far merely an adventure story and that was all.

"The cruiser—it came?"

"The cruiser never made the rendezvous. It was lost en route. And after that the whole affair went to hell." Fail-

90

ure—any kind of failure—did not please Bobby Blessing. He filled his teacup with rum and drank it down without pausing.

"The gold," said Dana, "disappeared into thin air. There was a massacre at the transfer point. The gold vanished. Someone in the operation knew those molds were solid gold. But how? Either by wit or because he had been told. Perhaps some of the cosmoline rubbed off; perhaps he could distinguish by weight . . . there are a number of possibilities, all presupposing either a traitor or a technician or both."

Blessing was calmer now. "The Brits sent survivors of their team down there year after year—matter of honor with them. As each appeared to get close to the answer he was murdered. Lassiter was the last. We were friends from the old days. He must have been getting close this time for them to set the dogs on him, poor bastard."

"I'm so sorry. And the Russians?"

"Naturally they know about the lost gold and they'd like to get their hands on it to finance their campaign to upset the western powers by backing the Coalition. Terrorism is expensive. The Russians don't want to show their hand publicly by passing out funds, so they encourage the Coalition to do its own fund raising, and they even help out now and then. We know they've lost agents in the Marseille region. And it's obvious they've inspired the Mitzu Brigade to go on the hunt for the gold."

"Because they were at Lassiter's?"

"Exactly. We believe somebody overpaid Mitzu to eliminate Lassiter . . . murder for hire is one of their fund raisers, of course. Mitzu got suspicious—the area was right . . . the victim was right . . . the history of the other dead Englishmen was right. They scented the lost gold. Hence the sacking of Lassiter's house. Hence your kidnapping and interrogation. . . ."

"Hence everything. Hence you wouldn't let me leave Aunt Lydie's—trying to protect me. And the murder of the ambassador . . . that means the destabilization plan is beginning here?''

"The activities of the Coalition change what might have been purely a British affair into everyone's affair. If the Coalition's agents get their hands on that half billion dollars," Dana said, "they can buy weapons like. . . ."

"If they get their hands on that more than half billion dollars before we do we can all begin to imagine the unimaginable." Blessing stamped out his cigarette furiously. It crumbled into black dust from the frenzy of his attack.

Dana had a faraway look. "I think she can imagine."

And the president was traveling to France.

"Is a submarine safe?"

They didn't think it was a foolish question. "There's a new weapon. . . ."

"For sale?"

"Everything is for sale if you have the price."

I didn't want to hear any more. I slipped down in the bed until the comforter touched my chin. I closed my eyes.

"It's been too much for one day," Dana whispered. "Let's go. Let her rest."

He was right. It had been.

I heard them tiptoe out. I heard the door close. I think, surprisingly, that I slept.

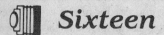 *Sixteen*

I slept off and on all that day and into the next. When Hannah, Aunt Lydie's personal maid, appeared with my

92

breakfast tray I found that I felt like a new woman. I was definitely clear-headed, definitely strong, definitely cured.

And I realized that I had definitely forgotten to tell Blessing and Dana about Praha and what I'd learned.

Now Dana had disappeared again and Blessing wouldn't be back until evening.

Aunt Lydie was around, though. She popped her head in just as I'd finished my bath and was pulling on a pair of white cotton jeans.

"Oh, excuse me, Persis. I'm glad to see you're up and about."

"So am I, Aunt Lydie." I pulled on a white knit shirt and went to the dressing table to examine myself in the mirror. I looked a little thinner, but otherwise none the worse for wear.

My aunt stood behind me and examined me with a quizzical eye. She was done up in a beige and white Chanel suit. Ropes of pearls and gold chains cascaded down the front of her white silk blouse. Her handmade Italian shoes, I noted, were also beige and white.

"Persis," she said, "don't you ever wear skirts? You have such attractive legs."

"Not practical," I told her. "I'm a working girl."

"You young people—always practical. She's wearing trousers, too."

"Who's wearing trousers?" Aunt Lydie is a mistress of the non sequitur.

"The young person waiting to see you downstairs. She's called every day since the ball . . . since you've been out of commission. I didn't realize that you were such good friends."

"What young person, Aunt Lydie?" Sometimes she could be maddeningly vague and this was one of the times.

"The child who's married to that cross-looking man, Hallsey Bryce."

"*She's* waiting to see me?" I couldn't imagine it. I don't think I'd spoken to her more than five or six times.

"Indeed she is. What a dear little thing—so concerned

93

about you. And parked right here on the doorstep this morning. I think the least you can do is to see her, even though she does wear trousers. I've put her in the morning room.'' And she went dashing off, heels beating a bright staccato on the hallway floor, calling back something about having to do some shopping and then back for an appointment and then to the races because she had a horse running. A few seconds later I heard the Austin Princess start up in the cobblestone courtyard and knew she was on her way.

I put on my lipstick and went downstairs to see—what was her name?—Nathalie Bryce.

"Good morning. Aren't you nice to come see me."

She jumped up when I came in the room. I'd always thought her an uninteresting looking little thing: her eyebrows almost met over the bridge of her nose, her features were not refined, her body tended to be stocky. When the bloom of youth was gone she would be in trouble. All these things were obvious to the artist's eye though probably not yet visible to anyone else. And today she was not at her best—she looked harassed and worried.

"Oh, Mrs. Willum . . . thank God!"

Her slacks were too red. Too baggy. Too long. Her hair was too short. Her shoes had those funny V-shaped heels the French were featuring this year. And her stockings were colored—the wrong color—too bright, almost purple.

But the odd thing was that there was something appealing about the disastrous nonorganization of her appearance . . . the kind of appeal one finds in a puppy that trips over its own feet and knocks things over with its wagging tail.

There was also something appealing about her perpetually worried look. Seeing her now, I realized that I had almost never seen her when she didn't look worried. There was in her appearance something of a lost child who is not entirely certain of his welcome at the first door he knocks upon.

Funny. A girl with a husband like Hallsey Bryce, who drove the most expensive cars and had bought one of the

94

most expensive mansions in Gull Harbor. What did she have to be worried about?

It didn't make sense.

"Oh thank God," she said again. "Thank God! He's out of town—I don't know where. Thank God you're here."

It seemed an unlikely thing to say. "Please call me Persis, Nathalie. What is it? Are you in trouble?"

Her hands were clasped together so tightly that her knuckles were white.

"I saw them take you away at the ball."

I was instantly alert. "You did? How did you happen to notice?"

"We were on the balcony. I saw you come in. I wondered how you would ever join the rest of us, it was so crowded. Then they took you away."

"I see. Why, exactly, did it worry you? I was just feeling a little claustrophobic."

"It worried me because. . . ." With absolutely no warning she burst into tears. They cascaded down her cheeks as if a dam had burst. Perhaps it had. She made no effort to mop up the flood.

I pulled a handkerchief from my pocket and went to the rescue.

"I have to leave him." Her face looked like a watercolor portrait someone had left outdoors in a downpour—all the features appeared to have run together.

"Here, blow your nose, child. And for goodness sakes, stop crying. You're not making any sense. Leave whom?"

"First it happened in Belgium. They were nice people. So kind to us. And a kidnapping. Hallsey was there on business for several months. He moved us to Norway. He was doing business with the government. Patents, he said. And again people were kind to us. Another kidnapping. Then Amsterdam. The same thing, only it was after we had come to America. I couldn't have stood to see again the fear and suffering."

95

It wasn't easy to understand her between the wrenching sobs, but I got the general idea. "Are you saying, Nathalie, that you thought I'd been kidnapped?"

"I can't tell you what I thought: I had to see you with my two eyes to be certain it was true that you were home and all right. I had to. Forgive me."

I have never seen a girl on the bare edge of a breakdown, but I was seeing one now. Her eyes were unfocused, her body totally uncoordinated. I put my hands on her shoulders, gently led her to the love seat beneath the window, and pressed her down among the pillows Aunt Lydie had needlepointed. They had little slogans. "Be reasonable—do it my way," said the one behind her head. "I'm perfect," said the one behind her shoulders. Aunt Lydie has spells of being domestic, but not very.

I sat down beside her and put my arm around her shaking shoulders. She buried her head in my white shirt and almost immediately I could feel wetness seeping through.

"I'm all right," I said. "You needn't have worried. They'd never kidnap me—nobody would pay the ransom."

"They didn't pay the ransom in Belgium and he was killed and dumped in the Wester Schelde. You don't know. . . ."

"Hallsey—your husband—surely you don't think. . . ."

"Think? I haven't been able to think coherently for months. I haven't been able to sleep. I wanted a father—I'd never really had a father. I thought he'd be everything . . . cherish and protect and love me forever. I would never have to worry about growing old—that was when father deserted my mother . . . she wasn't young any more. Hallsey was so much older . . . I would never have that fear. Fear? I never knew what fear was until now."

"But what do you fear?"

There was a long silence. Finally she spoke. "I fear *him*. I fear him because things happen where he is—nasty things. Seeing you being dragged out of the KIKI Klub decided me. They can't all be coincidences. Whenever we make an

96

effort . . . 'be nice to them, Nathalie, they're important to me.' 'Smile, Nathalie—it's a man who likes young girls.' 'Go sit with the gentleman, Nathalie—he has a fondness for nymphets . . .' '' Her shoulders heaved, and I thought for a moment she would be ill all over me and my now soggy whites. But I held her tight and gradually the rise and fall of her shoulders subsided.

I looked down at this child in my arms and thought how wonderful it was that she cared enough to be certain I was alive and well.

"When I saw them taking you . . . you were the only one in this whole place, aside from Madame Milonsky, who has bothered to be nice to me and *she* doesn't like my clothes . . . I had to know that you were all right. You understand?"

"I do. And as you see, I'm all right. What about you?" I hadn't thought about this girl for two consecutive minutes before. But now it was suddenly important that she should be safe.

"I'm leaving tonight. Marcel will take care of me. We're leaving for the south of France. He's making a film—Marseille is headquarters for his studio. It's cheaper, he says. And more agreeable. He has an apartment on the Boulevard Longchamp and later his yacht will come over and we'll live aboard her in the Old Port. At least he's young. And maybe, just maybe I'll get to star in a film."

Did she *know* what kind of films he made? Some people never make the right moves. But who was I to criticize? My life was a tapestry of wrong moves . . . a disaster of wrong choices.

"I hope you'll be happy." I was certainly the last to judge. But Martin?

"Please, don't tell anyone. . . ."

That she suspected Bryce of having people kidnapped? That she was running off with a porno king? They would think I was mad.

97

"Don't worry, Nathalie. I won't. But please let me know. . . ."

"You can reach me any time. Number eighteen, Boulevard Longchamp . . . I've already memorized it. It's going to be fun. I haven't had any fun for so long. . . ."

"I'm sure you will."

I walked to the door with her and watched her cross the courtyard to her gray Mercedes. She climbed in and then turned and waved to me.

"Good-bye!"

"Au revoir."

But I couldn't help wondering if what I should have been saying was *"Adieu."* It has an entirely different meaning.

It means, literally, "to God."

As I waved good-bye to her a yellow cab whirled into the courtyard, missing the Mercedes by inches.

Seventeen

It isn't every day that a great painter has need of advice, but apparently Nadia Milonsky did. And she must have needed it desperately, because she was inviting me to her studio, which had been off limits for as long as anyone could remember.

The message, delivered by hand by the Gull Harbor taxicab Madame employed for all her minor errands, arrived as Nathalie's car departed. It was scribbled in gigantic felt-tip pen letters on the inside of a flowery get-well card. Madame, obviously, was not fussy about her stationery.

98

I'm just back from a flying trip abroad to discover that I'm in the throes of painter's block. I've looked at the current portrait and I HATE it. Worse, I can't CURE it. Never happened before. Help! Cab will transport you to and from.

Nadia M.

Naturally I hurled myself into the cab: it never even occurred to me to say "no." I was so flattered I would have run there barefoot. Not even Madame's sitters had been inside that studio and when she entertained it was always at one of the Gull Harbor clubs. "Darlings, I hope you don't mind . . . my house is such a hovel." Work that required the actual presence of her sitters was executed in their own houses. Madame did the finishing touches privately in her studio, working from photos and without the presence of her clients.

As a sometime portrait painter myself, I could understand how it might happen—even to someone as skilled as the countess. It happens to every painter sooner or later . . . there you are, painting happily away after a lifetime of successful portraits, and suddenly one of them goes bad and everything you do only makes it worse. You don't dare show it to the unfortunate subject—you're sure your career will be ruined. You work and rework it: it only gets worse. There's only one solution, finally, and that is the one Madame had chosen—bring in an experienced, outside professional. Nine times out of ten he will put his finger on the problem. Even more important, he won't talk.

So here I was on the way to Nadia's. And I owed it to my experienced eye and my reputation for discretion. I was thrilled. In my field Milonsky was a giant: to be invited to help her was like receiving a summons from Jupiter.

The cab turned on to one of the modest streets in mid-village. We were in the little area that constitutes Gull Harbor's "downtown"—home of the Gull Harbor Chemist, the Country Boulangerie, the Village Store, the Book Nook,

99

the Full Glass (the most important merchant in town), and one or two other chic little enterprises necessary for the daily existence of the citizens. The taxicab dodged into a space between Never on Sunday (a lingerie shop) and the Big Cheese and there we were—in another world. Sitting behind neatly pruned privet hedges were a dozen or so unostentatious houses guarded by the square of shops around them like the interior of the Alamo by its walls and blockhouses. It was an area most of Gull Harbor didn't even know existed.

The cab deposited me in front of number twelve. "This is it," said the driver. "My orders are to be back for you in half an hour." The taxi drove off in a flash of yellow.

Milonsky's house was also yellow, but the genteel shade of watered-down lemon juice. It was encased in aluminum siding and surrounded by altogether unenthusiastic plantings of the most anonymous kind.

A manservant of indeterminate age greeted me at the door and led me without comment through a decently appointed living room and down a small hall to what must originally have been a downstairs bedroom. It was now Madame's atelier.

Madame was addressing her easel when I stepped in. She was addressing it with the gritty ferocity of a racing helmsman addressing the tiller of a recalcitrant sailing yacht.

"Damn—this portrait is going to finish by driving me mad. A disaster! I need your help, Persis. Where have I gone wrong?"

She stepped back, almost bumping into me, and threw out her arms in a gesture of martyrdom and despair. Specks of paint flew off her brush and splattered the canvas. She didn't seem to notice.

The atelier still had the air of a bedroom. There was no skylight, no sink, no linoleum floor. Instead there were two very ordinary windows without curtains and a clothes closet on one wall and tired looking green wall-to-wall carpeting.

100

It was obvious from the carpeting that Madame was a neat painter despite her splashing brush. Obviously she was in the grip of fierce frustration at the moment.

Only the big studio easel in front of her and a high, upholstered sitter's chair—currently occupied by a spread-out and draped man's three-piece gray suit—proclaimed the room's true identity.

Propped on the easel was a portrait of Hallsey Bryce. It was more than half completed. Pinned to the back stanchion of the easel directly above the painting were several photographs of the subject which the artist was using for reference. In the photos Bryce was wearing the three-piece gray suit that was draped across the chair. The clothes were present: the sitter was not.

I studied the painting. If she wanted my help, she would get it, and honestly. I took my time. And as I looked, little worms of unease began to wriggle beneath my skin.

"What have I done?" she was asking. "I'm suicidal. This has never happened before. I've lost it and I can't get it back. Please tell me—where have I gone wrong? You know the man."

The ten-by-eighteen canvas had a hand-carved Hydenrich frame already placed around it, a trick employed by some portrait painters because they believe it easier to imagine the final result with the frame in place. On the wall opposite was a large mirror, another painter's trick: when things go wrong it is sometimes helpful to look at the canvas in reverse, as reflected in the mirror. Often unsuspected flaws show up in the mirror image.

I saw the problem almost at once. Without realizing it, she had caught the evil and corruption and viciousness of the man who was Hallsey Bryce, qualities he didn't show in public but that Nadia Milonsky's brilliant intuitive talent had reproduced without her even being aware of what she was doing. The result was a portrait that was alarming— actually frightening. But how could I explain? What could I tell her?

I found the portrait so loathesome that my eye strayed from it as I tried to form the words of a critique that would be helpful. Seeking respite, I gazed at the photographs thumbtacked on the easel. Bryce in profile. Bryce full face. Bryce three quarters. Different poses; different lights. Strange, disturbing, masterful photographs. Something tugged at the back of my mind. What was it?

"It's a wonderful painting, Madame." Might as well take the plunge. "No question of who it is. But . . ." I paused, still searching for the right words, "I think the smile is wrong. I think that man has a sinister smile . . . and you've caught it. Perhaps if you toned it down—although it looks just like him—it's certainly his smile . . . but I hate it . . . in person, I mean. . . ."

She was already working with the brush. In a dozen strokes the smile was gone. It changed the whole portrait. Bryce no longer looked like a decadent monster reveling in the spectacle of an enemy being burned at the stake.

"Magnificent, Persis. You've saved my life. By all that's holy, I'm grateful. You put your finger exactly on the problem. I never would have found it. Look—now he's the real Bryce . . . a bit cold, perhaps, but not so . . . weird." She was wearing a blue satin smock and I noted that there wasn't a speck of paint on it. Poor thing—she had really been in a state over the Bryce likeness.

"It's brilliant. Perfect."

The impressive nose twitched at the compliment and she sat down heavily on her painter's stool and gestured again with the sable brush. "That canvas over there against the wall . . . turn it around. I'd like to know what you think of it, as long as you're here and you've been so kind."

It was a finished portrait on a stretcher and not yet framed. The subject was Courtney Lassiter and the likeness was so good it was like coming face to face with the man himself.

"Madame—it's the best thing you've ever done."

She allowed herself to preen a little. "You think so? It

102

does catch him, don't you think? I admit it. And by the way, he's never seen it completed. Have you heard when he'll be back? I've asked around but nobody seems to know. I don't understand. He promised. . . .''

She went no further: she didn't have to. I understood it all: her insulting remarks about him . . . her conversation with Cochran. She and Lassiter *had* been lovers and she thought he'd gone off and deserted her. Her call to Cochran had been a fishing expedition to see if Cochran knew his whereabouts. She was in love, and she feared she was a woman scorned.

I felt sorry for her, but what could I tell her? I had given my word.

And there was still something more. Something about those photographs. The artist's eye. . . .

"I don't know. Perhaps you could ask Bobby Blessing? He knows everything that goes on in Gull Harbor."

"I have, naturally. Nothing."

Lassiter and Milonsky—lovers. My head was spinning. Could it be possible . . . at their age?

But I knew it could.

And I knew I had to change the subject. I couldn't go on lying to her, pretending I knew nothing. I took a deep breath and looked frantically around the room. My eye lighted again on the suit Nadia had placed on the sitter's chair. And suddenly it clicked. No, it couldn't be . . . absurd. But, unbidden, the image of a Cossack formed in my mind.

I spoke without thinking. "What happened to the book?"

"Book? What book?" She wasn't alarmed, merely distracted. I don't think she really heard me.

"Parisian Nights."

This time she heard. I had the impression that her whole body chemistry had stopped dead—no pulse beating, no blood coursing. I think that reaction was what confirmed it.

"I saw you take it." Unable to stop now. "I was in the dressing room." The book. The photographs.

103

There wasn't even a tremor in her voice. "What exactly did you see?"

"I saw you put it inside your tunic and leave."

"You think I am a thief?"

"No." Of course she was not a thief. She was something else—and the explanation was in front of me, tacked to the easel that held Bryce's portrait. "I think that before you were a portrait painter, Madame, you were a photographer." The answer was there before me.

The great face began to crumble.

I pointed to the photographs of Bryce. "No fancy lighting or lenses, no special equipment, no tricks. Yet they are obviously the work of a genius—obvious, at least, to the eye of another artist, though maybe not to anyone else."

"No."

"In those days young women did not wander the streets by night—not if they were nice young women. So you turned yourself into a man to be able to go where you wished and photograph the city as you loved it—by night. As a man you could venture safely into the darkest alleys of Paris." She was tall. Turning herself into a boy would be easy. Hair pushed up under a cap . . . baggy clothes . . . her camera. . . .

"What you say is ludicrous."

I went on, like a runaway horse. "Then came the attacks on you and your book. You disappeared. Eventually you came to America, as a painter—we all know that for the truly gifted, one form of talent melts easily into another. You were comparatively safe here—who would believe the starving boy-photographer of Paris in the thirties was the great Madame Milonsky? But you are Praha, Madame. I know it now."

She pulled herself together, standing very tall and looking me straight in the eye. "No one will ever believe you."

"I do not intend to tell anyone."

"I would deny it. When I was Praha I was young . . . thin . . . timid . . . gentle . . . self-effacing. Today I am

104

the opposite. Who would ever guess, except you? How *did* you guess? Was it the book? It had to be the book. You guessed when you saw me take it."

"That was the beginning, I suppose. Who told you Martin had it?"

"Cochran, in one of our chats." Her features were regrouping.

And I'd thought Cochran's words were for me alone. "Where is the book now?"

"I destroyed it. I hope it is the last copy in the world and that I can now count on dying in my bed of natural causes. I intend to be buried in my best St. Angelo clutching my Renaissance silver hand mirror and a magnum of Perrier Jouet." She glanced at her wrist watch. "And now the cab will be waiting—it is time for you to go. I have another appointment."

I gave her my hand. I was really giving her my pledge. "I promise that I will say nothing. You have my word."

"Of course." She smiled. "No one would believe you, anyway. No one would care. I would deny everything and they would laugh at you."

She was right, and I knew it. And anyway, it was an old story. Who would care?

Then I remembered.

Lassiter had cared.

He had probably said something to her like, "Darling, I'm off to the south of France for a bit of business. I'll be back before you know it." Lassiter, never knowing she was Praha.

And Milonsky, waiting for a return that never happened, had mentioned it to Cochran, hoping for a scrap of information. Milonsky, who never dreamed that Lassiter would be on the trail of Praha once he was in Marseille.

The irony of it haunted me all the way home in Nadia Milonsky's yellow taxicab.

▥ *Eighteen*

Nadia Milonsky. Praha.

I crouched in my corner in the back of the cab and tried to get my wits together.

Should I have guessed the moment I saw the countess in her Cossack costume? Should I have guessed when she bridled so at my suggestion, made at the airport, that she might use photographs in her work?

Should I have guessed when Cochran told me she was the source of the information that Lassiter was in the south of France?

But how could I have guessed? I would have had to be some sort of genius to put it all together.

No—it was the theft of the book that told me finally. And the beauty of the photographs she had taken of her subjects. But only someone like me would guess from the photographs—only an artist. She was safe.

Because I would never tell. It was her secret and mine. She was a great artist twice over . . . a magnificent photographer and a superb painter. She was special. She was worth lying about to protect because the magnitude of her talent placed her above and beyond the rest of us.

I had given my word and it was sacred: I would never tell.

The yellow cab passed the entrance to Von Berger's estate and just on a whim I asked the driver to stop for a minute. The place was called "Fechtende Trappen," as if to advertise the glorious news that Von Berger was of Ger-

106

man extraction. Fechtende Trappen boasted the usual long Gull Harbor drive to the main house, but with few leaves yet on the trees I could see through to the front turn around. Three Mercedes were parked there—two black and one light blue. With so many cars in evidence I deduced that I had a good chance of finding the airplane dealer in residence.

I was right.

A very military-looking aide opened the door and ushered me into a small paneled library to await Von Berger. He appeared in a minute or two, splendid in a pale blue V-neck sweater, gray flannels, and a yellow silk foulard embroidered with his initials.

"Mrs. Willum—what a pleasure." He was bending over my hand and I had a fleeting moment of panic over whether my nail polish was equal to the honor.

"I was just passing and thought I'd call on you. It's still one of the old-fashioned customs here."

"Very European—a custom I'm happy has not died."

"What a lovely house you have. It used to belong to friends of my parents. I spent many happy hours here as a child." I looked around me, remembering those times. I would certainly never have recognized the house today—it was as different as if it had never existed before. Everything was dark, ornate. The furniture was heavy oak; the single painting over the mantel portrayed Germanic ladies sporting about in what I assumed to be the Black Forest. The bookcases on either side of the fireplace contained not books but lead soldiers. From the unfamiliarity of some of the uniforms I assumed they dated from early Germanic wars. I definitely recognized several by the spiked helmets of the Kaiser's troops in World War I and the distinctive field uniforms of the German troops and officers in World War II.

Von Berger let me look while he lounged gracefully against the fireplace. He was, I confessed to myself, definitely a good looking devil. Not only was he tall and courtly and blond, but he had a neatly defined head and the arro-

107

gant bone structure of . . . of what? What was it that nagged at me?

"I see that you are a war buff," I said, looking at the shelves full of models.

"*German* war buff," he admonished politely. "My family were always military people, traditionally fighting officers in command of combat troops in the Imperial German Army. They fought under Frederick the Great. They served Bismarck. They died in World War I at Verdun. And my father did his duty in the last great war."

In other words, I thought, his father served under Hitler. But if he was a professional military man, what else would he do?

"I see. And you?"

He laughed. "My family is now dead . . . I was devoted to them. But they are gone. So I . . . I am a citizen of the world."

"You prefer not to live in Germany?"

"I prefer not to live next to the Russians, if you please. I do not mind working in Europe—I am there constantly on business. But I prefer to live here, in the United States, because America is the hope of us all." There was nothing melodramatic in the way he said it: he might have been discussing the breakfast menu, he was so matter-of-fact.

"And how did you happen to choose Gull Harbor?"

He shrugged. Even when he shrugged the motion was graceful. He threw out his finely-made hands in a gesture of amusement. "Who does not know of Gull Harbor? It is true that I knew no one in Gull Harbor when I first arrived, but I find that it is very easy to make friends—particularly in America. Americans are so generous with their invitations that in the few weeks I have been here I am sure I have met everybody I ought to know."

I'll bet you have, I thought.

"Does your business take you often to Marseille?" I asked.

His eyebrows rose over the pale, pale blue eyes. "Mar-

108

seille? But of course—I go there occasionally on business. Why do you ask? Can I do anything for you when I am there the next time?''

I stood up. ''Yes. Bring me back the true Marseille recipe for Tapinade, if you please. I had it once when I was there with my aunt and I loved it.''

''I am not very interested in food,'' he told me coolly, ''but I will try to remember.'' If my mention of Marseille had startled him for a moment, the intentionally frivolous request had reassured him, though not before I received a message: whatever he did with this aircraft, it was not totally honest—at least when he was dealing out of Marseille. Was it there that he conducted illicit business with Third World powers, supplying them with bombers and pursuit planes? Was I letting my imagination run away with me?

I didn't think so. There was something about the way he carried his head. He looked like a very beautiful bird of prey.

''Well, thank you for receiving me. And welcome to our simple little community.''

He got the joke. ''Thank you,'' he said, laughing.

''And I love your house. What does the name mean, by the way?'' We were at the front door now and I pointed to the wrought-iron foot scraper with Fechtende Trappen lettered on it in small gold letters. I had noticed that even the rugs and draperies were made of a design created from the initials F.T.

''Fechtende Trappen means combat troops,'' he told me proudly.

''I see. Well, good-bye.''

And all the way to The Crossing, on the final leg of my yellow cab journey, I kept thinking about that, too.

▥ *Nineteen*

The Crossing was in an uproar when I returned. A gold and white van was parked at the door. "Van Clef et Fils, since 1867" was lettered on its side. It was brand new.

Aunt Lydie's favorite jeweler had arrived.

Inside there was turmoil. The staff was running about as if the world were expected to come to an end in the next fifteen minutes. Small dogs were yapping. My aunt was seated in the library issuing commands. No one seemed to be listening.

I tried to creep past without being observed, but a man I'd never seen before motioned me in. Aunt Lydie was excited.

"Persis—at last. Where have you been? I was halfway through my errands when I remembered that Mr. Ruinsky was coming today so I could select some new jewels for the Paris festivities. Mr. Ruinsky couldn't come himself, but he has very considerately sent his son and a whole new group of people to take care of me."

Mr. Ruinsky was the actual Van Clef of Van Clef et Fils and always had been. For thirty years he had been coming in person with a king's ransom in jewels for Lydia Wentworth to examine. It was always the same scenario: he arrived in an unmarked, bullet-proof car with a beautiful lady assistant and an armed bodyguard who remained present throughout. These encounters were marked by a certain pallor on both sides: Aunt Lydie blanched at the thought

110

of the vast amounts of money she was about to spend—jewels were her fatal weakness—and Mr. Ruinsky paled at the prospect of the vast amounts of money he was about to make. Both, in short, were always in a state of anticipatory bliss.

Today my aunt was exhibiting her customary pallor. Ruinsky *fils* wasn't pale but he seemed jumpy. His father would never have approved . . . it was one thing to be pale with anticipation but never, by so much as a tremor, should the jeweler betray a sign of nerves. It is of paramount importance that a merchant peddling priceless jewels give the impression that the current transaction means nothing because there are many more eager buyers in the wings. It's part of the game, part of the mystique. It's how you get people like Lydia Wentworth in an acquisitive mood. Sweet indifference had always been Ruinsky's strong card, the card that unfailingly persuaded Aunt Lydie to open her checkbook.

But this young man was jumpy. It was apparent in the brusque way he motioned me into the room, eyes scanning the hall behind me. He didn't look or act the least bit like his father.

Nor did his two armed assistants follow the Ruinsky tradition: both wore dark glasses. *Père* would never have approved of that because it gave them an ever so slightly sinister look. With the father in charge, the guard had been so unnoticeable as to be almost invisible. Invisibility inspired confidence when such transactions were taking place.

There was also the obligatory lady assistant on hand. I had never seen her before, either, and she was a far cry from the elegant black-clad lady who was usually in attendance.

"Young Mr. Ruinsky insisted on waiting for you," my aunt said. "His father has been ill and so he has sent the whole second team today. I suppose it's a sort of try-out for you?"

Ruinsky *fils* nodded curtly. He motioned to one of the

111

guards, who left the room swiftly. I heard the front door open. I heard his footsteps as he checked the courtyard.

My aunt was still talking. "His father told him you have a perfect eye, Persis, when it comes to selecting jewels that look well on me. In fact I think I do remember saying once that I would never spend more than fifty thousand dollars without asking your opinion."

I could see that the customary jewelry madness had so taken possession of her that a bomb in the courtyard wouldn't have caught her attention.

"I don't remember anything like that, Aunt Lydie."

"Neither do I, to tell you the truth."

"I thought not."

"In any case, I love having you here to give your opinion. This red dress—ordinarily I think red is rather vulgar but this one is an exception. I absolutely will *not* wear anything vulgar in Paris—I owe it to Jiggs and Marianne to make a good impression. The French think we have no chic—we must disabuse them. And the jewels must also be exceptional. What do you think, Persis . . . rubies? Rubies and diamonds? Diamonds alone?"

She signaled one of the parlormaids who had been pressed into service. "Please hold the dress up to Mrs. Willum. Someone put the rubies around her neck."

The *vendeuse* approached with a three-tiered ruby necklace. For several instants it dangled splendidly right before my eyes. Then it was clasped around my neck.

"Aunt Lydie. . . ."

"No—it won't do. So difficult to decide." She held up the other two necklaces and studied them fiercely, frowning with concentration. Ruinsky *fils* was fidgeting. Aunt Lydie didn't notice—she was too involved with her jewels.

"Aunt Lydie. . . ."

"I can't seem to decide. . . ."

Then I realized: she wasn't wearing her contact lenses. They were a recent addition to our lives, one she deeply

112

resented and chose to rise above as if her vision were perfect.

The front door closed and the guard came back into the room. He exchanged glances with Ruinsky *fils*.

"We always serve tea when Mr. Ruinsky comes—why not have some now? I'm dying for a cup." It was the first thing I could think of.

Lydia Wentworth adores life's little ceremonies. "Perfect! Your father always had a spot of sherry, too. And some little sandwiches, Jennings. Take the maids with you and see what you can do, quickly."

Jennings gathered up the maids. The younger Ruinsky seemed pleased. "I'll send my men to help."

Jennings started to protest, but I broke in. "Yes, do." Then in a low voice, as the disapproving butler passed me, "And be sure that the new chef includes the finger sandwiches."

Ordinarily Jennings is the most inscrutable of butlers, which is to say that no flicker of expression is ever allowed to cross his face. The present chef had been with my aunt for fifteen years, so there was a twitch—just a small one—of surprise. Then he marched out of the room followed by his little entourage of maids and men.

Ruinsky had produced his gun. It didn't surprise my aunt: his father, too, had always been armed. After all, he was carrying a king's ransom in jewels. She just rattled on.

"Now that that's settled, would you step into the powder room and actually put on the dress, Persis? I must see it *worn*. You don't mind, do you Mr. Ruinsky? Your father always let me do it this way. I like to match the gown and the jewels, you know."

"Miss Sherman will go with her." He seemed to be listening, but not to us.

"You think my niece will steal the rubies? Your father never minded: he knew my niece—jewels mean nothing to her."

113

He didn't answer. I realized he was listening to the group as they trooped downstairs.

My aunt shrugged and for the first time cast him a curious glance. "As you wish."

Miss Sherman and I stepped into the powder room.

It was by no means an ordinary powder room. In fact, it was by no means an ordinary room. The walls were covered with Vertes murals. The furniture was glass and steel Art Deco. The rug was hand-hooked by George Wells to match the deep blue and silver of the upholstery and curtains. These touches were all Aunt Lydie's, dating from her Art Deco period. But the most astonishing touch was the contribution of her grandfather, the old tycoon A. K. Wentworth. On his European travels he had seen and fallen in love with Botticelli's *The Birth of Venus*. Being unsuccessful in his efforts to purchase the original, he had settled for commissioning copies of every size to be hung in each room of his Gull Harbor mansion. The job had kept several painters busy for several years. His granddaughter had long since thrown out the paintings, but his mania had not stopped there. At the same time he had commissioned Italian sculptors to do ten-inch-high bronze reproductions of the Venus to serve as water taps for every bathroom in his house. The basins were in the form of shells and Venus was flanked by two angels for faucets, also in bronze. Some of these fixtures were still in working order. The one in this room was in poor condition, the Venus in place but only loosely: she was waiting to be repaired.

"Do you mind if I wash my hands before I touch the dress? I'm a bit grubby—it's been a busy morning." I didn't wait for permission. Miss Sherman didn't look as if she'd give it. She looked to me like a lady who wouldn't be too fastidious. Maybe I had that impression because her fingernails were too curved and too red. Ruinsky *père* would never have approved.

I went to the basin and turned each cherub. Water came out from beneath the miniature shell on which the Venus

114

stood and ran softly into the larger shell of the basin. I put my hand on the Venus.

"Miss Sherman . . . would you please check the hem of that dress before I step into it? I thought I noticed it coming undone. . . ."

Miss Sherman bent over. I lifted up the Venus and hit her on the head with all the force I could command. She crumpled without a sound. I took the dress from her, holding it over my arm to hide the heavy bronze Venus.

"Mr. Ruinsky . . . something's happened to your assistant—come quickly. She just toppled over—like that. Come!"

He was wary, motioning with his gun for my aunt and me to precede him. Aunt Lydie looked puzzled and started to protest, but thought better of it and obeyed. When she saw Miss Sherman on the floor she cried out in distress. "Oh, I hope she hasn't been ill on my rug . . . the flu . . . everybody's been ill . . . I hope. . . ." She rushed forward and tried to turn Miss Sherman on to her back.

Ruinsky motioned her away. "Don't touch her. Just get back."

He leaned over, gun still in hand.

I lifted the Venus. A round cry of protest formed on my aunt's lips, but she never uttered it: the look I gave her would have silenced an entire Greek chorus.

The Venus struck again—harder than ever. It was the strength of desperation.

And Ruinsky dropped. It was a miracle. I thought we'd both be dead and instead there he was, draped across his assistant's body, their arms and legs mingling in an intimate but disorganized tangle.

"Persis," my aunt was crying, "have you gone mad? Attacking my favorite jeweler's son just as I'm about to make my selections?"

"He's not your favorite jeweler's son. You just weren't paying attention. No class. And too nerved up. And his men are busy right now tying up your staff downstairs. We

115

need the curtain cords from the library . . . will you please get them?'' I had Ruinsky's gun and Aunt Lydie went obediently to fetch the cords, rather—I imagine—to her own surprise.

"I don't understand," she complained as we rolled the false Ruinsky off the false Miss Sherman and proceeded to tie both of them up in knots. "Why isn't he my favorite jeweler? Isn't he the 'Fils' of Van Clef et Fils?"

"He is not," I told her, pulling tight a final loop. Neither victim of the bathroom Venus had budged; but they would soon. "We have to hope now that Jennings will set off his mad contraption and that help will arrive before those hoodlums come back upstairs. I know that Bobby Blessing assigned men to patrol the grounds after the ambassador's death."

"What mad contraption?"

"The New Chef."

"Oh my goodness!" She was remembering. Jennings had never trusted our conventional alarm so he rigged up his own anti-burglar system. The main ingredients were a button and a tape recording magnified to sound as if the house were under attack by the whole of Patton's Fifth Army. For months whenever we couldn't track him down he had always said he was busy with "the New Chef."

And just then the New Chef went into action. The cacophony was ear-shattering. Even I, who knew it was only the New Chef in action, was almost persuaded that our number was up.

"Come on, Aunt Lydie, let's go up to your room and bolt ourselves in until help arrives."

"But the jewels," my aunt cried. "I wanted the rubies and someone might steal them."

"Don't worry," I said. "They were copies. Good—but paste copies. You should have worn your glasses. I spotted it at once. Ordinarily you'd have noticed."

"Oh." Very embarrassed. "How could I have missed it? Is that what put you on to them—your artist's eye?"

116

"That—and their lack of class—Ruinsky would never have sent them out to represent the firm. Never."

"But. . . ."

In the midst of the New Chef's bombardment I now heard sounds of real gunfire. Then there was the roar of the van starting up and hurtling down the driveway. And shortly after that Blessing's voice. "Lydia . . . Lydia . . . where are you? Are you all right?"

"He's come," my aunt said. "I'm glad." A masterful understatement.

"But what did they want, if the jewels weren't real? I don't understand."

"I do. I understood the minute I realized they were waiting for me. They didn't want any surprises. You were about to be kidnapped in their fancy new van. *We* were. I was getting a free ride."

"You're not serious. Kidnapped? How idiotic."

"I know," I told her. "Why do you suppose I was desperate enough to hit those people with your grandfather's beloved Botticelli Venus?"

"I don't know. Why? I simply thought you had gone mad."

"Because," I told her, "I knew you'd *never* pay the ransom and I'm not ready to die."

She had the grace to look shamefaced; but she didn't contradict me.

▥ *Twenty*

The scene between Bobby Blessing and Lydia Wentworth that followed our deliverance was a classic battle of wills.

117

Blessing was determined that Aunt Lydie should go into hiding where she could be properly protected from further kidnap attempts. Aunt Lydie was determined not to.

"I have all my preparations for Paris with Jiggs and Marianne: I don't have time to go into hiding, as you call it. Furthermore, it's an absurd idea. I've made it patently clear on many occasions that I will *never, never* agree to the payment of ransom."

"All very well, Lydia . . . but suppose they began to chop Persis up, bit by bit? An ear here—an eye there. Would you not send permission to your bankers under such pressure? Why do you think they waited for her?"

She thought about it. "They wouldn't dare. If they were caught. . . ."

"You'd better believe they'd dare. And suppose that didn't work: suppose we received one of your fingers—say that one, complete with ring. Do you think we'd hesitate to beg or borrow the money to get you back? Why are you so obstinately refusing to see the danger? What use will your money be to you if you are dead, and Persis, too?"

"I'm leaving it to orphans, and retired and homeless horses. It will do good for many years."

"Homeless horses! Really, Lydia—you can't be serious."

"I've never been more serious. I will not . . . I repeat *not* . . . pay ransom to anyone." She was utterly unshaken by the kidnap attempt: perhaps the reality of it had not yet dawned on her.

But Blessing did not surrender. "All the more reason, then, to see that you are not kidnapped. I've been working on a plan for weeks. I believe we could leave tomorrow morning. We will fly to Gatwick on one of those tourist flights—no one would ever suspect it was you and the flight is not uncomfortable."

"What did you say?" My aunt had never traveled less than first class in her life: she obviously couldn't believe her ears.

118

"It won't be bad, I promise," Blessing continued. "Then we'll take a small plane to La Baule where we'll be met and driven to Batz-sur-Mer. I've rented a large, quite wild-looking seaside house there—big enough to give you and Persis each a private floor and still leave plenty of room for my men, who'll double as servants."

"A tourist flight? I've never taken one." She had a faraway look in her eyes, like a child contemplating a whole counter full of forbidden candies. "I think it might be fun. And could we stay in a motel? I've never been in one. I'd like *that*, too."

Blessing didn't yet realize that he had her hooked and continued to unroll the details of his plan. "You'll be an English lady for this occasion: they're used to the English in that region and your accent isn't the least American. I think you'll find Batz amusing: they harvest salt, and there's the sea. We chose it because the house is well protected and because they're accustomed to the English renting big places for the season, which is almost upon us."

"June is the beginning," I said. "It's not yet June."

"I know. But we've put it out that one of you is an artist who likes to paint the sea in all seasons."

He'd been very thorough.

"I've never seen salt harvested," Lydia Wentworth said.

"You'll be on the Côte Sauvage—the Atlantic side: it's pretty spectacular. And if you can't live without the sophisticated shops and restaurants, there's La Baule nearby. You'll love it, Lydia. I've spent a good deal of thought on finding you the perfect place. And there are the fishing fleets of Le Croisic. . . ."

"I've always wanted to go out on one of those bright-painted fishing boats," she said.

"It could be arranged." Blessing understood now that she was seduced. Like all the small international company of super-millionaires, she always went to the same chic places. But unlike them, she was endlessly curious about the rest of the world and hampered by the fact that people

119

in her exalted tax bracket could not move about like the rest of us.

"How long will I have to stay?"

"No longer than it would have taken for you to get your Paris house in order. You'll be on hand in plenty of time to greet Jiggs and Marianne. By then the kidnappers will have turned their attention elsewhere: they need money *now:* we know that."

She looked delighted. "You mean you want me offstage just long enough for them to forget about me and concentrate on somebody else? All right—I agree. I'm not at all anxious to be dragged off in a van by types in moustaches and dark glasses. As long as you guarantee I'll get to Paris in time. . . ."

"You will."

They both looked relieved that the contest was over. My acquiescence was taken for granted by both sides.

▥ *Twenty-One*

Batz-sur-Mer, in Loire-Atlantique, Brittany, is a curious small town popularly believed to have been founded in 945, a town in which no one in his right mind would expect to find Lydia Wentworth, one of the wealthiest women in the modern world.

To begin with, it is a smallish, unpretentious place into which the sea has tentatively intruded shallow fingers to probe the surrounding fields. There are no great houses, no fine restaurants, no chic boutiques. The streets are narrow, the houses simple. On the Atlantic side, the ocean lashes mercilessly at the high cliffs and barren rocks that guard Batz from its fury. On the protected bays, the land has been cultivated for salt beds, and at the outskirts of the village housewives set up tables and place displays of their bagged salt on them, along with great sacks of potatoes and onions fabled for the special taste attributed to the saltiness of the surrounding fields. On weekends the roads leading from Batz are clogged with motorists stopping to buy the villagers' wares.

Aside from its salt, potatoes, and onions the village has just two other claims to fame: a large bronze statue of a beautiful Breton girl striding in from the salt marshes with a basket of salt balanced on her head and—just across from the church—a sabot maker whose flamboyant gifts as a promoter bring customers from miles around to buy his wildly diverse variety of wood-soled shoes.

My aunt fell in love with Batz-sur-Mer on sight. So far we were batting one hundred percent—she had also fallen in love with the economy flight to Gatwick and with the erratic small plane that flew us from Gatwick to the rainswept airfield at La Baule, near Batz. I prayed that her good humor would last. We still had one hurdle to negotiate: her personal maid, Hannah, refused to fly and would not be with us for at least a week. In Paris Aunt Lydie always had a spare maid in attendance until Hannah's stately arrival by boat and train. In Batz, for the sake of security, there would be no personal maid but me. I did not anticipate that I would be a success.

Actually, there was one other hurdle, one that I also dreaded. Would she like the house—she who was used to every luxury and comfort?

I needn't have worried. The eccentric pile of timber and cement . . . a concoction that resembled a French chef's wedding cake gone mad . . . delighted her. She loved the cliff. She loved the crashing waves at our feet. She loved the corridors and fireplaces and beams and parquet floors. Even the heavy furniture delighted her. "It's a true *maison*

121

de maître," she exclaimed. "I've always wanted to live in one and now I shall—at least for a while."

"Do you really think you'll be happy here?" I was thinking of Hannah and how Aunt Lydie had not even packed her own pocketbook since she was a little girl.

"I'll be in seventh heaven. How do you pronounce this place? Batz as in baaaah as in sheep?"

"Yes."

"Extraordinary. I shall never master French pronunciation."

I was unpacking. Aunt Lydie was sitting on the edge of the bed, swinging her foot like a child.

"Why not put the gloves in that drawer . . . I'll never need them here. And the lingerie there. And by the way, what was in the package that taxi delivered just before we took the plane?"

That's the way she does things—delivers her blows when you're not looking.

"Oh." I thought frantically. I didn't realize she'd noticed. "Nothing."

"Nothing?"

"Well, just something from the gallery. Work. Gregor must be losing patience with my never being there."

She giggled. "I wouldn't worry if I were you."

I knew what she meant. If it pleased Aunt Lydie to have me trot around with her for the rest of her life, Gregor would be the last to object. He was mad about her.

Finally the unpacking was done. Not well, but done.

"Now that we've finished, I think I'll take a little beauty rest." She yawned.

"Exactly."

The package was lying where I had left it, on the bed in my room next to my pocketbook. It was about eight by ten inches in size, wrapped in plain brown paper, and tied with bright yellow kitchen string. Altogether an unimposing affair.

But I had a feeling . . .

As I touched it my heart began to beat a rousing tattoo.

122

It had arrived at literally the eleventh hour, delivered by Madame Milonsky's cab. I had carried it carefully in my hand from America to England, from England to France without once daring to look inside. I knew she would expect me to open it in privacy.

And finally I was alone.

My fingers trembled as I untied the string.

The wrappings fell away. There was tissue paper—layers of it. And finally . . . photographs.

They were black and white. They were not of Paris, I saw that at once. It was a different city. A different time and a different mood. There were girls. Soldiers . . . German soldiers. Boats. Bars. Wartime.

I saw the name of a bar, barely distinguishable in the light of a street lamp. "Café de la Canebière, Marseille."

Marseille. Praha had been in Marseille. It was not possible to mistake Praha's work . . . not possible to mistake the quality.

There was a note, penned in the usual flamboyant hand on the usual commercial greeting card. This one said "Happy Father's Day." And she had scribbled "These are safer with you. Use as you see fit. I trust you. You will know what to do. And when to do it."

And that was all.

I went back through the photographs, studying them, searching for a face that might be familiar, the face of a murderer. No face stood out. There was nothing.

I looked at the note again. "You will know what to do."

But what was that?

123

▥ Twenty-Two

The eight days before Hannah's arrival were a sort of idyll in which my aunt and I dwelt together in bucolic simplicity and pastoral charm. We took long walks along the littoral (followed at a discreet distance by Blessing's guard dogs). We lunched at a charming little restaurant looking out on the breakwater. We counted the fishing boats at Piriac-sur-Mer and La Turballe. We strolled the beach at La Baule, bundled up against the spring winds and marveling at the young men already pitting their *planches à voiles* against the still-cold seas. We ventured to Pen Bé for *moules* and *huîtres*, plucked fresh from the ocean. We tasted *le salicorne*, the strange grass grown in the salt marsh beds. We dined at the three-star restaurant Bellevue Plage in La Baule and strolled the medieval streets and ramparts of Guérande. And one day, in an excess of ecstasy, we almost climbed aboard the three-story rococo merry-go-round in front of the Hôtel Royal in La Baule.

My aunt was like a child in a fairy-tale dream. Never once did she complain about my clumsiness as a drawer-of-baths, mixer-of-martinis, layer-out-of-clothes-for-the-day.

Never once did she chafe at the bit Blessing had imposed upon her—from her sunny disposition and total contentment one might have thought the sojourn in Batz had been her idea, carefully orchestrated for at least a year. She was amiability unparalleled to the guardians assigned to watch over her—even when her plans conflicted with theirs. It

124

was, I finally decided, a reaction to the stresses of having the ambassador murdered before her eyes and almost being kidnapped, two events shocking enough to unsettle even so emotionally adjusted a person as my aunt. I kept telling myself that it was too good to be true and every day I woke up wondering if *this* was the day that would shatter the idyll. But nothing happened. She was charm itself.

Even the *International Herald Tribune* and its unsettling world news failed to upset her, although there was a slight tremor on the tranquil surface of our lives when an article appeared headlined: "WHITE HOUSE ALERT EXPLAINED. Security was tightened at the White House last night in response to intelligence reports that terrorists were planning a major attack on the American president, either here or abroad. . . .''

When she read it, Aunt Lydie (who had herself insisted that the security men drive to La Baule every morning to buy a copy of the *Trib)* threw the offending newspaper across the room. "Take it away," she cried. "It's a plot to keep Jiggs from the conference. They're trying to intimidate him! But he'll never submit to threats. I know Jiggs. He'll be in Paris, no matter how they try to scare him off. He's a great president and he'll be there to protect the western world. You can count on it.''

That was the only flurry of excitement—otherwise the days passed without upset. If it rained, she loved the rain. If the sun ventured out she was enchanted. Every meal was bliss. She drank Gros Plant, the local wine, and pronounced it marvelous. She ate her first galette in her first Crêperie and adored it. She bought eight pairs of shoes from the sabot maker and ordered five more. I wouldn't have been surprised to wake up some morning and find her clad from head to foot in the local Breton costume.

And I could do no wrong in my role as Hannah. Although I was clumsy, inept, disorganized, forgetful, and totally inefficient, Aunt Lydie was all-forgiving. One would have thought she had stumbled into Paradise. Even Bobby

125

Blessing's ever-present troops failed to annoy her with their presence.

But she knew the day would come when she would go to Paris: perhaps her pleasure was heightened by the knowledge that she would soon be wallowing in luxury in the company of some of the most powerful people in the world. Soon Hannah would arrive, soon Paris would call. And off she would troop, carefree and gay and quite forgetful of the unpretentious pleasures of Batz-sur-Mer which had given us refuge from the trials of our recent life on Long Island. My aunt could never resist the luster of the City of Light for very long. But then, who could?

In the meantime, here we were. It was restful and it was safe. But it was like being in prison. Everywhere we went, every waking hour I thought about Lassiter and Praha and the whole mad affair. What was it that Praha expected me to do? What?

I puzzled over it day and night, spilling my food, stepping into holes, almost being run down by cars in my foggy, distracted state. If my aunt noticed, she didn't say anything. Probably she attributed my worse than usual absent-mindedness to my efforts to serve as a competent ladies' maid.

"You will know what to do."

I studied and restudied the photographs.

Why couldn't I work it out?

Twenty-Three

I suppose I would have gone with Aunt Lydie to Paris; we all took it quite for granted that I would. But the telephone call from Bobby Blessing changed that.

It must have been after lunch in New York because we were about to dine in Batz. My aunt likes to dine late.

"I have bad news," Blessing said. He was never one to feint if a straight blow to the jaw would suffice. He sounded as if he were in the next room, which made matters somehow worse.

My aunt motioned to me to get on the *écouteur,* that fantastic French invention which enables two people to listen, but not speak to, the caller simultaneously.

"What bad news, Bobby? Are my investments in trouble?" Naturally she associated bad news with finances: it was ever thus with people of superior means.

"No. No . . . never better, as a matter of fact. No—it's Nadia Milonsky."

I think my heart, for all intents and purposes, stopped beating. I didn't want to listen to what was to follow, but I listened anyway: I didn't know how to stop.

"Nadia? What has happened to her? Jiggs doesn't like the portrait she did of him?"

"Nothing like that, Lydia. I only wish it were. Far worse, I'm afraid."

"What could be worse for a professional portrait artist?" My aunt was being pragmatic but not imaginative.

127

"She's dead." He dropped it like that—without hesitation, without mercy.

"Oh, no." I could clearly hear in my aunt's tone the words "not this, too."

"I'm afraid it's true, Lydia."

"How?" She could scarcely ask the question.

"A senseless business. The police speculate that hoodlums broke into her house and, when there was no money to be found, killed her and that old man who worked for her and her secretary."

"Hoodlums looking for money? In Gull Harbor? You can't mean it." There had never been hoodlums in Gull Harbor. It was unthinkable. "There must be another explanation, Bobby."

"There isn't, I'm afraid. We think the secretary tried to oppose them and everyone was shot. The place was torn to bits—the police say they've never seen anything like it. Don't worry—she died instantly . . . a shot in the back of the head. The secretary and the old man were trying to defend her. Nasty business. I wouldn't have called, but I didn't want you to read it in the paper tomorrow."

"Do you think I should fly back?"

"For the funeral? Definitely not. I absolutely forbid it. It's the last thing Nadia would want—to put you in danger. No, Lydia . . . that's one of the reasons I called. I was afraid you'd read about it in the European press and insist on taking the next flight back. You must not do that—not under any circumstances. I absolutely forbid it."

"But I ought to. . . ."

"No. You're always so kind and generous. But this is one time when you must think of yourself first. Under no circumstances are you to return. It is too dangerous. I will not permit it. You will remain where you are. I will attend to the flowers and whatever else is necessary. Nadia would be the first one to understand—she was a European, after all, and Europeans know the value of life and the folly of risking it needlessly. No—you will not return. Hannah will

128

be there in twenty-four hours and then in a few days you can go on to Paris to prepare for the president's visit. That is important.''

He had said all the right things.

"I suppose you're right, Bobby—you always are. I've traveled all this distance because you wanted me to. I might as well stay because you want me to. You'll take care of everything?'' She looked quite shaken.

"Of course.''

"Good. Then, if you wish, I'll stay until Hannah comes and until you say it's safe to go on to Paris." I think Nadia Milonsky's death actually had frightened her—I'd never seen her so docile. I know it frightened me.

"Very good, Lydia. It won't be long—I promise you— maybe a week or so. I'll call and let you know when it's safe. My men will go with you—they'll take over at your Paris house.''

"Very well, Bobby. Thank you." All three of us hung up.

"I'll wait until he tells me I may go," my aunt said meekly.

"Yes.'' I was glad she had promised him.

But I couldn't believe it. Hoodlums behind the Big Cheese? Robbers behind Never on Sunday?

Never. Never in a million years.

Nadia Milonsky was dead. How could it be? I had been with her only days before and she had been so strong, so vital, so alive—promising to die in her bed of natural causes and be buried with her mirror and her Perrier Jouet.

How was it possible? Could it be. . . .

Beauty and the Beast. The masks that hung over me, asking—always asking. Had I told them I'd seen her take the book? Had I?

Had I assisted at her death without knowing it? And she'd trusted me. "You will know what to do.''

My aunt was looking at me in alarm. "Persis—are you all right? You look terrible . . . as if you were about to be sick. What's wrong?''

129

"I wish," I told her, "that I could die. Right now." And I began to cry. It was a shocking display: we don't blubber and moan in Gull Harbor. But I couldn't help it.

〗〗 *Twenty-Four*

I had been in Marseille before, of course. But the circumstances had been different.

On those previous occasions I had arrived like a princess, stepping off a yacht in the Old Port with my aunt. Together we had dipped our elegantly painted toes in the vitality and excitement and implied danger of one of the most electrifying cities in the world . . . dipped our toes without ever getting them soiled. We had strolled the vast Canebière in our wide-brimmed summer hats, goggling at the crowds and drinking the refreshing juice made from grapes pressed before our eyes. As the streets darkened and the humming markets folded their wares we had returned to the sanctuary of our floating palace to drink champagne and admire the glittering lights of the city of sin and crime. This time I was arriving like everyone else, by a fast French train. It was all very fast: the sudden decision, a note for Aunt Lydie, a train from La Baule, and I was gone. I had telephoned ahead from Lyon to make certain that Nathalie Bryce was in town and, just as I had hoped, she had immediately insisted I stay with her. "You can walk from the station."

I studied the thickly carved doors of the Napoleon III town houses for the correct number. From the brass plates on many of the doors I had the impression that the area, while certainly far from run-down, had definitely seen better days. Many of the buildings now housed doctors and lawyers and individual apartments. Number eighteen, when I found it, was no exception: a brass plate informed me that the bureau of Martin Films, Executive Offices, could be found on the first floor. Martin *privé* was listed for the rest of the town house.

Nathalie met me at the door, looking radiant. Life with Martin evidently agreed with her. The pudgy face had been done over by someone with cosmetic know-how to dramatize cheekbones and eyes. She was a different girl.

"You'll stay here—we keep rooms for visiting VIPs and potential investors and they're all yours for now. From your bedroom you have a beautiful view of the golden Virgin that guards the city from the top of Notre Dame de la Garde."

"You're too kind."

"Not at all—I'm lonesome . . . Marcel is away all day and so far I haven't been offered any parts or even allowed on the set. Marcel doesn't want me exposed to pornography. He'd rather I stayed home and stared at the Virgin whereas I—for my part—would like some *real* excitement."

"The Virgin's pretty exciting—at least to an artist. She's more than forty feet tall and magnificently gilded and made of four hollow sections, an alloy of zinc and copper. Aunt Lydie and I climbed the circular staircase inside to get a view of the city through her eyes—literally. I'll take you . . . I think you'll find it exciting."

"Will you? And you'll have absolute privacy here to do as you want. But please join us for dinner. Marcel is looking forward to it. Every night, if you can."

"Gladly. And I have a favor to ask of him."

"He's very good about favors," she assured me solemnly. "In fact, he's very good about everything."

I sincerely hoped she was right. I was counting on it.

Could I count on Nathalie, too? I studied her, wondering. I needed an ally, but was she the one? My kidnapping,

131

the attempt on Aunt Lydie, and finally the murder of Nadia Milonsky had forced me here. There had been no choice and I think I had known it the moment I opened the package with Praha's photographs. Nadia Milonsky had counted on me—believed in me. The arrival of the photographs had sealed the unspoken pact.

But whom could I count on? Martin? I needed him, surely. But could he be trusted? Nathalie? No, not possible—she was a child, an immature girl begging for something exciting to happen. I could give her that. But it wouldn't be fair.

"Show me the house, Nathalie. It looks beautiful."

She shrugged. She was used to wonderful houses. "I'm having my favorite decorator flown over. I don't like the way the place is done. I suspect all of Marcel's mistresses had a hand in it. They were mostly actresses, you know . . . and actresses have no taste."

Her lower lip jutted out in disapproval. Recalling how badly she had dressed in Gull Harbor, I quailed at the fate of the house. Still, as she gave me a tour of the place, I could see what she meant. Everything in every room was expensive—that much was obvious. But the melange of objects and tastes was staggering. I felt I was drowning in a sea of gilt and mirrors and armoires and tapestries and upholstery of conflicting patterns doing battle with oriental rugs of furiously disagreeing colors. Purples and dark greens and bright yellows and deep reds swirled before my eyes. There were puffs of brocade everywhere. Tassels. Fringes. Pillows and geegaws. It was enough to give you vertigo.

"A decorator. What a good idea." Any decorator would be preferable to the present state.

"It will give me something to do. I'm so bored. Marcel says I'm to have a free hand. He doesn't notice things very much."

Obviously. Or he couldn't have lived here.

"That's very nice of him." I sat down on a Louis seize chair with gold painted legs. Nathalie sat opposite me on a dark red Empire sofa under an oriental six-panel screen mounted on the wall. The screen was mostly orange and brown and dark green. Crystal lamps with silver shades flanked the sofa. There were two side chairs opposite done up in bright purple with cabbage roses in the design. I began to feel quite ill: it had been a long day.

A Vietnamese houseman served Pastis.

"He was a colonel at Dien Bien Phu," Nathalie offered. "Marcel rescued him from the Foreign Legion. You know that their headquarters are in Marseille."

"I know." It was one reason I was here.

"Marcel," she offered proudly, "is like that. He knows everybody."

"I suspected that." It was another reason I was here. "And are you happy, Nathalie? Is it working out? You're not sorry you left Hallsey Bryce?"

She looked better, certainly. And she seemed better. But one could never be sure. All this talk about excitement. . . .

She didn't answer directly. "You'll find Marcel is different once you get to know him. Not like Hallsey. Different. But still, you know, all men are the same in the end." She smiled at me and it was the crooked smile of a little girl, which didn't at all match the worldliness of what she had just said.

Her mood changed abruptly. "Finish your drink and we'll go down and take a coffee in one of the sidewalk cafés and watch the world go by. Because that's where the world is—in Marseille. Did you know that Von Berger is here? And I wouldn't doubt that Hallsey was here, too, searching for me and spying. Maybe we'll see them. And then, when we're thoroughly bored, we'll come back and dine with Marcel. No one dines before nine—so we have plenty of time. And whatever favor you have to ask of Marcel you can ask over cognac. He'll not refuse you, Persis . . . he's never been known to refuse a lady."

Von Berger and Bryce? Impossible. Too much of a co-incidence. Still, if I was here, why not everyone else?

I put down my Pastis and jumped up. "I'm ready. Let's go."

As it turned out, we saw about a thousand people in the course of drinking three or four coffees.

But none was Von Berger. And none was Bryce.

Twenty-Five

Martin looked natty in a pink silk shirt, white foulard, white flannel slacks, and white buck shoes. Blinding, in fact.

"Did you know," I asked as we lingered over cognac after dinner, "that Nadia Milonsky was murdered in a robbery?"

"Appalling—we read it. The news was in all the papers. After all, she's an international figure. Odd, though—no photographs of her."

"She never allowed them to be taken. She was very private."

"Robbery—imagine. In Gull Harbor!" Nathalie was scandalized by the idea.

So was Martin. "I never thought, when I bought a house in Gull Harbor, that such a thing could happen there."

"It never has before."

"She didn't even get to start my portrait," Nathalie complained sulkily.

"She more or less finished the rest of us but Nathalie's wasn't even begun. I don't suppose you'd consider . . . ?"

"Not really. I'm not a portrait painter, Marcel. It's a

134

now-and-then thing. I'm a *painter*. That's different. But I could suggest. . . ."

"I only want the best for her. As a favor, perhaps?"

The girl interrupted. I knew what she was thinking: I wanted a favor—he wanted a favor. "Excuse me, I must discuss tomorrow's marketing with the cook. She shops at dawn to get the best of everything." She left us, her silk caftan rustling mysteriously.

When her footsteps had died away, Martin lit a cigar and turned to me. "Why are you in Marseille? I, after all, have business here. But you . . . people like you don't come to Marseille."

"I came to see you, for one thing."

A short laugh exploded. He didn't believe me. "You're joking."

"No. In your profession you deal with a variety of people, do you not?"

His black eyes widened slightly. "I don't deny it. So?"

"Some of those people might help me."

"Oh? How?"

"A friend was killed here this spring." No one in Gull Harbor was supposed to have known where Lassiter was and Martin certainly wouldn't have met him—he was a late arrival in our community and Lassiter was long gone by then.

"I'd like," I continued, "to know why."

"All right. But why me?"

"Because you might have access to people who have heard something. Marseille is headquarters for the greatest of all mercenary armies, the Foreign Legion. It is made up of all types—criminals, murderers, escaped convicts, political *personae non gratae*—people of all kinds. Someone in that milieu must have heard *something.*"

"I see. Anything is possible. His name?"

"Courtney Lassiter."

"Ah, yes, Lassiter. What happened to him?"

"He was shot eight times at close range."

135

Martin allowed a long, slow whistle to escape. "Like that."

"Yes, like that."

"Information is hard to. . . ." he stopped. Nathalie had returned and was standing in the doorway.

"Who has been shot eight times?" She was just a little breathless, her kohl-rimmed eyes round with interest.

"No one, *Chérie*. We are discussing a possible plot for a film. Persis has presented me with quite a good idea."

"Oh." She sounded disappointed. "I thought maybe it was something real. Nothing exciting ever happens." She turned and went back to the kitchen. He waited until she was gone to speak.

"Any idea why he was in Marseille?"

I realized that I didn't really know. Something to do with the Marseille-Menton-Manosque triangle . . . something to do with Praha, with the gold. But what, exactly? I realized that I also knew next to nothing about Lassiter himself. "No."

"Well," Martin said, "the trail's cold, I'd say. But I'll make you a bargain. If I find out something useful for you, you will paint Nathalie. Agreed?"

"Done."

We shook hands. His handshake was strong and firm.

"I'll ask around," he told me. "But don't expect much, and not instantly—it will take a few days. Anyway, I'm relieved: there had to be a reason . . . people like you don't come to Marseille." He laughed the same short laugh, like a firecracker.

I studied him with interest. "You're an enigma to me, too. It's strange—you're not at all what I would expect."

He blew a mushroom cloud of cigar smoke and watched it ascend laboriously to the ceiling. "Why is that?"

"Well, for one thing, you don't look or act like a man whose occupation—or is it vocation—is pornography. You're too nice. You've been kind to Nathalie."

He laughed again. "Pornography is a business like any

136

other. I inherited it from my father, you might say—he was an agent for the kind of seedy and kinky acts that played the *boîtes*—the nightclubs—in the twenties and thirties. The natural evolution was pornographic films. We film them here because in Marseille it's easy to pick up people who will do anything for a buck. We market the films in Europe. America is just now becoming ripe for these things.''

"Is that why you bought a house in America?"

"No—not at all. Every European is trying to buy property in America . . . we all want our money there. Nothing in Europe is safe: we're on the brink of war. America is the only place to be.''

"All of you—you . . . Von Berger . . . Bryce?"

"Von Berger—there's a fellow who might help you. I saw him on the street the other day. Good looking fellow. Bones of a movie star. As for Bryce . . . there's a bad type. Mixed up with a gang of international criminals, I've heard. Finger man for terrorists. Just the fellow you need.'' He was smiling and his tone was heavy with sarcasm.

"Hallsey Bryce . . . he disappeared when he knew—" I stopped. There was no point in telling anyone that my aunt had nearly been kidnapped.

"That I was stealing his wife? Yes. But he did not make her happy. I shall.''

"I'm glad. She's a nice child.''

"I've been looking for just such a nice child all my life. A journalist who writes about crimes does not have to be a criminal. A man who makes pornographic films does not have to be a pervert. Does that answer your question?''

"It does. Now if you will help me . . . ?''

"I'll do my best. I'll try to find Von Berger—I've heard his father was a German officer who escaped into the Foreign Legion. I'll ask around among the people I know—as you say, I know a variety. I'll poke around in all the dark corners. And, if I succeed, you'll keep your part of the bargain.''

"I will.''

137

"Well," he said, "at least I'm relieved—my question is answered. As I said, people like you don't just come to Marseille."

"You may be right."

But then, neither did people like Courtney Lassiter. Nor, in the general run of events, did people like Nathalie Bryce or Von Berger or Marcel Martin, for that matter.

Everybody had to have a reason. And that was the question, wasn't it . . . the reason?

Twenty-Six

The next few days were not exactly calm. I rose early and returned late, between times scouring the photography shops and galleries from Aix to Arles and St. Rémy to Les Baux. No one had heard of Praha. But I thought some of the looks I received were peculiar. Or was it my imagination . . . was I becoming paranoid?

Nathalie came with me once or twice. But she soon abandoned the chase, mostly because she was under the impression that I was doing art research, and it bored her. But she was kind enough to lend me her speedy dark blue Peugeot in which to make my rounds.

I visited the bureau of the newspapers *La Marseillaise*, *Le Meridional*, *Le Provençal* and *Le Soir* in my quest for information. Nothing.

It was in a bookstore on the Canebière that I finally had an inspiration. They had a display of photographs promoting a new book and it gave me just the idea I needed. An exhibit of photographs by Praha . . . if it were well-adver-

138

tised, wouldn't it draw the murderer into the net . . . wouldn't he want to be sure . . . absolutely certain . . . wasn't it human nature?

I knew then—this was what I had to do.

I didn't waste a moment. I went immediately to the Musée des Beaux Arts. It was a logical beginning.

You have to climb to the top of the Boulevard Longchamp to get there. It is situated next to the Palais Longchamp, the climax to a stunningly Baroque series of cascading waterfalls and fountains topped by sculptured bulls and mythical marine figures.

I climbed the multitude of steps leading to the museum. I was starved: I had skipped lunch in my hurry to visit the Musée. The sight of a woman feeding twenty-two of the nearby zoological garden's wild cats, most of them kittens, honed my hunger and depressed my spirits. Suppose this didn't work? Suppose they weren't interested? What then?

I told myself not to expect too much. I knew that this museum was a treasury of early works, mostly from schools that have gone out of fashion and by artists now unmourned and unsung.

Still, it was a start.

Somewhat to my surprise the young director and her two equally young curators received me politely . . . maybe they didn't have many American visitors.

I had expected someone ancient, to correspond to the museum's collection—Petrus Paulus, Marius Engalière, Monnoyer, Francois-Marius Granet, Barrigue de Fontainieu. I had not expected children. Perhaps all the old curators had died off and been succeeded by their great-grandchildren. Nevertheless, the mention of Praha's name brought a quick reaction.

"Praha—we would give anything to see his work!"

"You've never seen it?"

"Never." That, of course, was scarcely surprising.

"Then . . . ?" How could they, buried in these archives, know of Praha?

139

They stood looking at me like three little boys. Their black hair was cut like boys' hair, their skinny little bodies were boys' bodies. They could have been three street urchins who had wandered into a museum by mistake. And they were as solemn as street urchins examining a stranger. After they had looked at me and then at one another they came—like children—to a wordless decision. "If you will tell us why you are asking about Praha, we will tell you what we know." I had the impression that we could be trading marbles. It was absurd—they weren't little boys—they were art people. But they were still people and they were curious.

"I have a small collection of his photographs. They were made in Marseille. I was hoping you could help me find a place to exhibit them."

There was one of those pauses that is described in books as a stunned silence. The three little boys exchanged glances again. "Not here," the director said. "We are permanently fixed in *le temps passé*. But . . ." She paused, considering. "It would be the perfect thing. Photographs by a great photographer . . . photographs of Marseille to celebrate the new work of the great choreographer Roland Petit, also a great artist, for the Ballet National de Marseille opening at the opera house almost at once."

"It could be done: we can arrange it," the two curators added eagerly. "They asked us what we could give them by way of an exhibition for the lobby on opening night."

"How soon?" It was right . . . made to order . . . perfect.

"Ten days," they chorused. "We were desperate for an idea."

"And now," I told them, "it is your turn. How do you know Praha?"

"No one ever knew him. But there is a reward for any information about him or about anyone asking for him." They nodded in unison. "One thousand dollars, we're told. Eight thousand francs—a lot of money. One hears these things in Marseille."

Was I surprised? Perhaps. "A reward offered by whom?"

"We understand it's a matter of a post box. And now we must ask—these photographs . . . their provenance?"

"They were given to me by the photographer himself, to do with as I saw fit. Look—here is his note. Every photograph is signed on the back. And you can call the Waldheim Museum in New York to check that I am who I say I am . . . here are my credentials." I passed them my passport and wallet.

They fluttered over Praha's note, which was what interested them. There isn't a curator in the world who doesn't thrill to the notion of a coup such as this. "When will we see the photographs?"

"Tomorrow. I will bring them here. But there is one thing you must promise."

Three cropped heads turned to me simultaneously. The French don't like making promises any more than anyone else. "Yes?"

"My name must not be mentioned."

They thought it over and could find nothing wrong.

"You received the photographs in the mail with that note from the photographer himself," I continued. "You must say that."

They crossed the viewing gallery and conferred beneath an undistinguished French battle scene from the early 1800s. Their whispered consultation sounded, in that great chamber, like the humming of bees in a distant field. Finally they were finished.

"All right," they said when they returned. "Agreed. *C'est tout?*"

"No—that is not all."

And I told them the rest. They were all smiles and full of charm—I was not to worry . . . everything would be done as I wished. I knew that they would be on the transatlantic phone checking on me the moment I left the building; but there would be no trouble; the prospect of getting

141

credit for having unearthed lost works by a lost artist would keep them cooperative. "Praha," I said to myself, "we have taken the first step."

▥ *Twenty-Seven*

I left the museum and walked slowly to Le Longchamp, the park that joins it behind the marvelous eighteenth-century fountains and charging bulls. It was a hot day, but in the shade of the park's flowering trees there was respite.

There was one unoccupied bench and I sank down on it. Youngsters bicycled happily on the paths around me. Grownups strolled by towing an endless variety of dogs. A miniature covered wagon full of children and drawn by four very small black ponies passed in front of me. I scarcely noticed any of it. I needed this time to think. My head was in a muddle. Things had to be sorted out. And here in the park, surrounded by laughing children and strangers, I might have the privacy in which to do it.

There were, it seemed to me, two different things happening.

First: the gold and everything that had to do with it. The gold had been stolen by someone unknown, and Lassiter, friend of Bobby Blessing, had been killed—together with six other colleagues—maybe more—in an effort to recover it. It might be safe to assume that, as they had all died near Marseille, the thief (or thieves) was still in this area. And I might reasonably assume that the $500 million dollars were also on hand.

Second: the Mitzu Brigade and the Coalition. This was

142

essentially a different affair, having to do with a conspiracy to disrupt and destabilize the existing western world, a plan that required unimaginable amounts of money. The two situations overlapped by the merest chance, the tiniest whim of fate, because the man who stole the gold wished to have Lassiter dispatched and, in doing what he had probably done in the previous murders, had engaged paid assassins—in this case members of the Mitzu Brigade.

But in his zeal he overpaid, and the assassins—thirsty for money—found themselves in the same hunt for gold as the British. And the Americans, who had been in it unofficially before Lassiter was killed, had joined the hunt officially the moment Jiggs was threatened and the ambassador was assassinated. It was no longer just a matter of recovering lost gold: it was also a matter of keeping more than half a billion dollars out of terrorist hands.

All of that I understood. It gave me a headache, but I understood it. Barely.

But what about Praha? How did Praha and *Parisian Nights* fit into all of this? It was easy enough to understand the destruction of the book and the photographer's subsequent flight into anonymity. But why had Lassiter written to ask me about Praha just before he was killed? Why the interest in him in Marseille? And what had Praha been doing in Marseille, anyway?

There had to be some answers soon.

And the exhibition at the opera house had to be the catalyst.

143

▥ *Twenty-Eight*

The next few days were divided between Nathalie and the museum, where I helped the director and her assistants draft press releases for the Praha exhibition.

Nathalie and I industriously climbed the Virgin to peer out through her empty eyes at the port and the city spread languidly below, basking in the heat wave that had struck the south of France. Afterward we sipped *un jus de raisin* (1.50 fr.) on the Canebière and took a vedette from the Quai des Belges with ten Germans, an enormous Boxer on a chain, and two little girls with gold bracelets on each arm, to visit the Château d'If, the fortress in the harbor constructed by François premier and converted into a state prison in the seventeenth century.

I had never stopped at the fortress, although Aunt Lydie's yacht had passed it many times. "Too touristic," she always said, watching the crowds that clambered over the island and gazing with horror on those who had brought their swimming suits and were frolicking in the water. But my sensibilities were not so refined: I was eager to see the prison made famous by Dumas's Count of Monte Cristo who was imprisoned there—a childhood idol second only in my esteem to Athos of the Three Musketeers.

With Nathalie I was idle and almost carefree while I waited—hoping that Martin would come up with something. We shopped for shoes—Marseille was a multi-colored sea of shoes. We took Pastis in the sidewalk cafés. One night we even went to the races.

But I was also working. The press releases had been drafted and were beginning to appear. "Famous Lost Photographer's Work Recovered.". . ."Mystery Genius Rediscovered". . ."Lost Photographs of Marseille Go on Exhibit for Opening of Petit Ballet." Suddenly the press was full of Praha. Reporters leapt on the story—it had glamour, mystery, art. Petit announced in TV interviews that he had once seen a copy of *Parisian Nights* and considered it a work of genius. Bookstores, newspapers, and even the museum were flooded with requests for information and a plethora of false leads about the location of copies of the book. Museums all over France combed their archives and regretfully announced that they could find nothing. Survivors from the world of arts and letters of the thirties were interviewed. Those who were not senile confessed that they had heard of but never met Praha. They recalled the affair of the destruction of the book. But that was all . . . and not very fruitful.

Then, too, there was the matter of framing the photographs for displaying. They had arrived in my hands in the simplest possible form—matted, backed by ragboard, and covered in polyethylene to protect the surface. The polyethylene was too cloudy for proper appreciation of the pictures and would have to be replaced by glass. The glass, in turn, required a frame. The museum, always—in true museum tradition—hard up for cash, spent a lot of time clanking around in its storerooms searching for frames that might be suitable. So far they had come up with nothing appropriate but the search was still on. And growing a bit feverish.

I left the details of labeling and documentation and installation to the museum staff, but even so there was a lot to do. The minute details of an exhibition are endless.

"But it's exciting," the director said, her short hair standing out from her head as if it, too, shared the general enthusiasm. "Usually it's so *dull* around here. All we work with is dead artists."

145

I didn't mention that Praha was also dead. I was the only one in the world who knew that. Or was I?

"It's exciting for me, too," I told her. "It must be the first time ever that these photographs have been on view. I feel like Christopher Columbus."

"Or Samuel de Champlain," the director said, ever the Gaul.

"Yes. Or Champlain." No point in inflaming the National Pride.

And suddenly Martin came up with something.

We had just finished dinner. Dessert had been a superb Algerian melon with Porto and I was euphoric—all food in Marseille seemed blessed with a special sun-drenched superiority that left me lazy and relaxed and scarcely capable of coping with high drama.

But that was what Martin was offering.

Nathalie had gone off to bed the minute coffee was served. "Forgive me," she yawned. "I'm so very sleepy. It must be the heat." We all felt the heat. But it wasn't that.

"I put something in her drink," he said.

"What!"

"We're going out. We have a rendezvous. And it's better if she doesn't know. She'll be all right in the morning." He might have been discussing the day's laundry, it was that cut and dried.

"You've found out something for me?"

"I think you'll find it interesting. Drink up. We're leaving."

There was an unseen vibration in the air around Martin that told me to beware, to pay attention, to guard my flank. Martin was still an unknown quantity. I had gambled on him.

We were in the foyer now. He rang for the lift. "All right, then. We're off."

The elevator arrived, hesitant as a debutante at her first party. He pushed me inside and pressed the down button.

"May I ask whom are we seeing?"

We were wedged in shoulder to shoulder in the tiny space. I did not find the proximity comforting. It was like rubbing shoulders with an iceberg.

"No names. And no questions." That was all.

The elevator, wavering slightly, continued its downward course.

"Can you at least tell me where we are going?"

"You asked," he said without bothering to look at me, "for my help, did you not?"

"I did," I admitted.

"Well, now you're going to get it."

The elevator stopped with a jolt and the door opened precipitously. But he blocked the exit. "There's just one thing."

I should have known there would be. There always is: it's just a question of what. "Yes?"

"I smell money in this—big money. You wouldn't be here otherwise. People like you don't come to Marseille. So it must be. And I intend to find out."

Money? I had thought I was here for Praha and even for Lassiter and six dead Englishmen—never for money. But hadn't it all begun with Czechoslovakian gold?

"Money? I don't know. . . ."

I never had a chance to finish.

"Well, *I* do. There's money. And plenty of it. And I'm going to get to the bottom of it."

He moved aside and allowed me to step out of the elevator. I stumbled and nearly fell, scarcely aware of where I was placing my feet, too alarmed to care.

He made no move to help me.

147

Twenty-Nine

The street was dark and so was the café. I thought I made out the paint-chipped name CAFE DU PORT, but it was so dark that I couldn't be sure. I wondered if someone habitually shot out the street lamps here and decided, rather to my surprise, that they probably did.

Where were we? I hadn't a clue. Martin had driven like a madman around and around the tangled streets of the city (most of them made one-way in a hopeless effort to unsnarl the traffic) until I was thoroughly bewildered and disoriented. For one second—fleetingly—I thought I caught a scent of fish in the air, so perhaps we were somewhere near the waterfront.

One or two dim lights shone half-heartedly inside the café. It can't be the Old Port, I decided . . . nothing is this seedy there. We must be in the commercial area—that frightening maze of warehouses where the tankers anchor.

I could see a clutch of men clinging to the bar inside, as if they expected it to submerge momentarily. They never relinquished their grip nor turned to look at us. Perhaps they were professional nonwitnesses. It was a frightening thought.

Martin led me swiftly past the entrance and around to the side of the building where there was another door. It opened into a long dark hallway that culminated, finally, in a blacked-out room. He guided me by touch to a chair against the wall, navigating by the faint light that filtered in from the single bulb that marked the outside door. The hall smelled. The room smelled. Everything had the rank odor of clothes that had mingled too long with very dead fish. My stomach began to turn. I was going to be ill.

Then I heard it, and all my queasiness vanished. It was the faint stirring that meant we were not alone.

"Marcel?" I asked.

"Just be quiet and listen. There are two of them. They will speak in French. Do not interrupt, if you please. And do not under any circumstances light a match to look at them."

Light a match? I hadn't smoked a cigarette in ages. But I wished now that I hadn't been so virtuous. I would have given anything to see who was in the room.

One of them had begun to speak . . . hurriedly, nervously, and in heavily accented French. At first I couldn't catch the rhythm of it and then my ear adjusted: the accent was German.

"I was stationed here with the Wehrmacht. That was a long time ago. Afterward, I was in the Foreign Legion but this was before. One night we were ordered out . . . it was early in January 1943 . . . and piled into trucks and driven fast as hell down the coast. Maquis, they said. But it was over when we arrived. I was sorry about that . . . in those days fighting was *Glückseligkeit*—happiness. But it was finished. There must have been trucks . . . tracks were everywhere. Freight cars were burning. Bodies all around— some in our uniforms, and that was a curious thing. It looked like there had been an ambush, and a bloody one at that. I ought to know—I've seen a few in my time. North Africa . . . Belgium. . . ."

Martin broke in. "Go on."

"Afterward there was the usual sweep of the Old Port for information. Every petty criminal was rounded up and interrogated. The rumor was that a British cruiser had been discovered lying off shore to pick up some kind of special shipment and that she'd been sunk and the shipment am-

149

bushed. But by whom? If it was us, why the round-up? Well, ours was not to question.

"Anyway, a special railroad siding had been thrown up there so the cars could roll in with their cargo, whatever it was. The rails went all the way down to the beach—I saw them. Marseille harbor was bombed that night . . . the word was that it was a diversion. And in a few days there was the round-up in the warren of apartments and holes in the wall of the Old Port. There always was when something went wrong for our side. Thirty men were shot. Their names were on a list.

"We always wondered what it was about that night. We never heard. But a British cruiser—it must have been something big. So I've never forgotten."

A new voice broke in—this time it was in the unmistakable accent of Provence, thick and rolling.

"We never knew. And we were there too, some of us. In 1942 the Krauts occupied Marseille. They interrupted our business, those of us who brought things into the port. You know—not strictly legal, you might say. The French authorities had always been tactful . . . they understood the principle of live and let live. But the Krauts . . . they had to regulate everything. Ruin our livelihood. So naturally, every once in a while when the Maquis needed a hand we helped out. It gave us a chance to even the score a little.

"We got a call: extra men were needed for a night operation loading a ship. But we were late for our rendezvous—we had run afoul of a German patrol on the way . . . the Germans were very nervous that night. The rendezvous was for a small beach below the hills some miles outside the city. When we arrived there were bodies everywhere. Germans were loading up the last of a convoy of trucks and dispersing. It had been a massacre. Our people were lying all over the place. One of the Krauts, the one who seemed to be giving the orders, grabbed a flamethrower and began to torch the boxcars, yelling orders. It was like hell itself—you couldn't believe it was real. We

150

hadn't been spotted yet—our orders were not to break cover until ordered. But at that moment some idiot jumped up and began to photograph the scene. We dragged the fool back down, but we'd been spotted and there was a lot of shooting before the Germans finally took off in their trucks.''

I had been told not to speak, but it didn't matter. ''The photographer—you knew him?''

''No. We were a motley bunch—a little of everything.''

I hadn't expected better. I tried to imagine it. A country gobbled up by the enemy. A strange convoy snaking across Europe, trying to escape to England. A British cruiser sailing for a secret rendezvous. Bombs falling on the city for a diversion. And a collection of Maquis and criminals and patriots marching through the night to the rendezvous point, only to be met by disaster. A reckless photographer. . . .

It was long ago and it had no reality for me. ''You—Wehrmacht—you said something I didn't understand. Bodies all around, you said . . . some in our uniforms and that was curious! What did you mean?'' Martin had taken my arm roughly to try to silence me. But I had to know.

There was a long silence and I was afraid that perhaps I would not be answered. But finally the German spoke again. ''Yes—it was a curious thing—I've always wondered. As I said, there were bodies all around. Most wore the kind of dark clothes the Maquis used at night. But others were in our uniform. Well, not exactly. Bits and pieces of ours. Maybe most wouldn't notice, but I did. I'm good at details—and I'd been in ordnance where you learn to notice military details. Things didn't match. Wrong jackets for trousers. Wrong caps for insignia. Mixtures of wrong decorations for wrong campaigns. It was exactly as if all the uniforms had been pulled out of a barrel and put on at random. And that's it.

''It's all we know.''

''You're sure?'' Martin demanded. ''What about the cargo?''

151

There was no response from either of them.

"What was it? Where did it go?" Martin wanted an answer.

But he didn't get it. They were through. "We never heard. We don't know. Nobody knows. Whatever it was, it disappeared into thin air. There wasn't even a whisper—a rumor. Just gone."

Martin threw out an explosion of profanities. It was greeted by silence. Finally he stood up. "Oh, what the hell. And I called in a lot of favors! Let's go."

I got to my feet and followed him. Once again nobody at the bar gave us a glance as we passed outside.

We did not speak on the trip back: I was concentrating on trying to commit every word I'd heard to memory and I suppose Martin was doing the same. We wheeled and cornered across the city, doubling back on ourselves and executing complex patterns that could have inspired Roland Petit to create a traffic ballet. When we finally pulled up in front of eighteen, Boulevard Longchamp, we still had not exchanged a word.

Martin went through the ritual of locking the car that was part of the privilege of living in Marseille. I watched as he put the hand-written sign *"en panne"* (out of order) on the dashboard and tested each door. "O.K. Let's go in."

We started toward the building. Suddenly he stopped and took me by the shoulder and spun me around. There was nothing polite about it . . . it hurt. "Don't tell me there isn't money in this . . . I can smell it."

I tried to pull away. His grip tightened. "I won't stop until I find out. You've got a partner, Mrs. Willum."

We went into the apartment, the imprint of his fingers still deep in my flesh.

152

Thirty

I did not sleep that night. Each time I drifted toward slumber I found myself sinking into a vortex of blood and flame and had to force myself awake.

Finally I picked up a book. When all else fails, a half hour or so of reading will relax the mind and permit sleep to take over.

It was a paperback I had discovered at the Canebière bookstore where I saw the photographs—something about Czechoslovakia—something I thought might serve as background. I read a few pages. It was very pedantic stuff, and almost at once the formula began to work . . . my eyes became heavy and the book kept falling on my chest.

I persevered. Read. Drift off. Read again. I was determined that when I did finally fall asleep it would be for the whole night. I didn't want to wake up a hollow-eyed, sleep-starved wreck of my usual self, which isn't movie star quality at best.

Read. Sleep. Read.

And suddenly I was sitting upright, eyes like cake plates.

Because there it was, right beneath my nose. "Praha is the Czechoslovakian word for Prague, its capital."

Praha—Prague. Nadia Milonsky was a Czech, not a Russian. She had created her Russian persona when she came to America. Just as she had created a large, noisy, bewigged, jewel-encrusted woman to hide forever the slim, shy boy-photographer she had impersonated long ago. Masterful. Who would ever make the connection?

153

I sat there in bed repeating the name over and over again. Prague. Prague. Prague. I had to convince myself that it was real. Because now I understood. She had fled to Marseille to lose herself in the teeming city . . . surrendering now and again to the irresistible impulse to photograph.

Now and then, as a Czech patriot and a French citizen, she probably helped the Maquis. Surely she had done so the night of the aborted attempt to save the Czech gold. It was partly a Czech operation: she was Czech. There could have been another photographer present, but I didn't believe it: it was Praha whose speciality was photographing at night.

Another part of the puzzle had dropped into place. I turned out the light, rolled over, and fell instantly asleep.

Thirty-One

The first order of business when I awoke was to call the museum. I was full of energy. I had never felt better. I wanted to dance, or jump over a wall, or run a fifty-yard dash. I felt much too good. I warned myself: be careful, Persis—now is not the time to break a leg.

The museum director was pleased to hear from me. She was full of news. Suitable frames had finally been unearthed and if I would come immediately the young curators, who doubled as secretaries, restorers (or conservators, as they preferred to be called), framers, and general slavies would frame everything and have it ready to hang in ample time.

"I was certain we had something that would be appro-

154

priate . . . things have been accumulating in this museum for about two hundred years,'' the director told me calmly. "It's just a matter of patience and searching. Never give up, is my motto.''

I was glad she was so cool. With the ballet opening just five nights away she had been shaving the details altogether too close for comfort.

"I was getting nervous.'' Maybe old age was creeping up.

"You needn't: we always manage in the end. But there is one thing we didn't anticipate.''

My heart did its usual upward leap to resettle in the middle of my throat, a sure sign something was about to happen. "What?''

"We have already started taking the photographs out of their protective backing and polyethylene wrappings and we find now that we're one frame short. There's an extra photograph: it was doubled behind another. We'll have to make a decision: one photograph will have to be eliminated. Can you come right over?''

"I'll be right there.'' I was already tearing myself out of my jeans and flinging my body into something more suitable for the streets of Marseille where, whatever they do and however they do it, the ladies always wear dresses. After last night's interviews, I knew it was important not to stand out in any way: Lassiter and his colleagues had made themselves conspicuous by their inquiries about the lost gold. And they were dead. I didn't want to stand out from the crowd . . . being dead did not appeal to me.

Thirty-Two

The director and her assistants were skittering around in the museum storeroom like three hens in a granary. Each wore a blue-and-white striped apron that covered both upper and lower body and barely missed sweeping up the floor. They were brandishing hammers, finishing nails, and jars of goldleaf paint in differing shades. Three three-star chefs preparing a banquet couldn't have been busier.

"At last!" cried the director, as if she had been waiting for hours instead of minutes. "We thought you'd never arrive. We must make a choice now."

"Where is the extra photograph?" My heart hadn't stopped pounding since the director mentioned it on the telephone. Praha had been present the night of the failed rendezvous with the British cruiser. Praha had stood up and attempted to take photographs in the midst of the melee. Praha had sent a packet of Marseille photographs to me, just before dying. Was it possible . . . ?

"Voilà!" they cried triumphantly in unison. Their voices were high and soft and delicate, even in their excitement. It is only after years of marriage that French women develop the voices of fishwives.

The photograph Praha had hidden was produced and thrust beneath my nose.

It was a night picture, of course.

But it was also a battle picture.

There wasn't any question—it had been taken the night of the battle on the beach. The back lighting, which gen-

156

erated dazzling contrasts of light and shadow, was produced by a blazing railroad car whose skeleton was clearly visible behind the flames. Bodies were scattered about at random and in shadow. Figures raced through the dark, guns ready, rifles leading bodies. Part of a truck was vaguely visible. They were there, those details, but they were essentially shadows to the scene.

All the photographer's energies had been centered on one man. He was center stage . . . a Shakespearian actor about to present a monologue. The flames behind him wrapped him in an eerie glow, like a heavenly body appearing to a saint in a vision. He was pointing his weapon directly at the camera, bringing the photographer into his sights before firing. It was a moment of frozen recognition between subject and cameraman.

But there was no recognition for me.

The main actor was back-lit. His face was in shadow. How frustrated Praha must have been, developing his film . . . how defeated by the lost opportunity. No doubt this was the best of what he had managed to snap that night on the beach—and it wasn't enough. The face Praha had tried to capture was a nonface.

And yet. . . .

I kept the photograph in my hand, lost in study.

There was something.

But what? It was impossible to make out the man's features. Impossible to establish an identity of any kind. So why did I have this feeling?

Something titillating. Something elusive.

I handed the photo to the director who was standing by, waiting for a decision. "We will not use this. And may I use your phone to call New York? I want to tell someone to come to the ballet. It is important."

I was already dialing Blessing's number. I heard the phone ringing in New York. He had to be there—especially with Dana gone.

But he wasn't, although it was barely six A.M. in New York.

"Mr. Blessing is out of town," his sleepy houseman told me, not impressed that this was a transatlantic call. He sounded outraged at being roused from his sleep.

"Have you a number where he can be reached?"

"I do not, but he may be checking in today—or maybe tomorrow. I'm not sure."

"When he does, will you tell him to call one of these numbers at once? And tell him I need him here in Marseille immediately." I gave him telephone numbers for and the address of the opera house and everything else l could think of.

"Very good. I will do my best."

I hoped he would: I had the feeling I would be needing Blessing, and soon.

There was still one thing . . . the most important one of all. The director finally mentioned it just as I was about to leave.

"I almost forgot. You made us promise to tell you if there were any requests to see the exhibition before opening night. There has been one request."

I had almost lost hope. "Who?"

"We don't know. The ballet received an anonymous donation of fifty thousand dollars in return for the privilege of viewing the photographs before dress rehearsal. The donor has expressed interest in buying the entire collection and the ballet wants me to welcome the benefactor in person. Another fifty thousand dollars has been promised this museum if I will; and we can use the money."

"Most interesting. Most generous." The bait had been set out and advertised: now it was about to be taken.

"So naturally I will be there."

"Naturally," I agreed. "And so will I."

"Ordinarily, as I promised you, you'd be welcome. After all, this donation would not be coming our way if it were

158

not for you. But there is a serious problem: it was specified that I was to be the only outsider present.''

"You are showing the collection before dress rehearsal?''

"Yes. One hour before. Privately. No one else is to be there.''

"*I* will be there.''

The director put the tip of the sable brush with which she had been retouching frames between her teeth and chewed on it distractedly. I understood her dilemma: was it wiser to safeguard the fifty thousand dollar donation to the museum, or did honor dictate that she allow me to come because it was the main condition I had exacted when I offered her the photographs?

Honor won. "All right," she said. "Six P.M. sharp on Friday. Promise you won't let anyone know I said it was okay.''

I would have promised anything. "Just don't give me away when you see me. I have a crazy idea.'' I laughed. It was a laugh of sheer nerves and tension.

She looked grim. "Fifty thousand dollars is no laughing matter. I hope we don't lose it because of you.''

"I hope not.''

But fifty thousand dollars didn't sound like much to me. Not when the stakes were over half a billion.

Thirty-Three

It must have been all the publicity about the Praha show at the Opéra Municipal that finally flushed Von Berger.

159

At least that was my theory.

He surfaced quite suddenly at the end of the day.

I had devoted the afternoon to Nathalie, driving her the ninety-two kilometers to Arles on swift autoroutes for a few hours' diversion. We parked in the Place de la République, lunched at the ancient Hôtel de la Cloître, and then visited the Musée Reattu on the banks of the Rhone to admire a collection of Picasso drawings. At least I admired them—Nathalie was not enthusiastic. "I don't understand them," she complained. "Anyway, Hallsey always said they were the attic-warmers of the future."

"Look at them with your own eyes," I advised. "Think for yourself."

She wasn't convinced. "I'll try." But it was obviously a failure. So we climbed to the Roman amphitheater and that was more to her taste, although what she really would have preferred was to have seen a bullfight taking place in it.

"I've never seen one."

"I hope never to see one," I replied.

"Well, an empty bull ring isn't very exciting."

Then she discovered the shops that ring the outside of the amphitheater, and that was exactly to her taste. She rushed into them one after the other, eyes alight and purse open. By the time we were ready to return to Marseille we were both laden down like two-legged beasts of burden. It seemed to me that she had bought everything her glance fell upon and I wondered if Martin wouldn't be furious when he saw the wild assortment of glassware and china and fabrics and pottery and other odds and ends she had acquired. But she didn't seem concerned so I wasn't either. All those mistresses must have accustomed him to orgies like this.

We got back to Marseille in record time and it was a good thing, because there it was—an invitation from Hans von Berger delivered by hand and written with an extravagance of flourishes on paper that bore an indecipherable

160

crest. Would we come by for a drink this evening at six P.M.? He would look forward to receiving us, he wrote, and gave an address on the Boulevard Prado. He had already been in touch with Martin, he added, and Martin would meet us there.

"We will go, of course," Nathalie said. "It's really the first interesting thing that's happened."

"Do you know his house?"

"No. But it's a very chic address, I think. Mansions and the Turkish embassy and goodness knows what else. *Très, très chic.* We must also be very chic. There will be wonderful people there. He has probably taken Marseille by storm since he has been here, no matter how short the time."

It was my guess that he had taken Marseille by storm many moons ago, for this was not his first visit. I knew that much from our conversation in Gull Harbor. And a man like Hans von Berger would never keep a low profile—not with his good looks and golden hair. Women were, after all, the same the world over. The ones with the killer instinct would ferret him out no matter where he tried to hide. And a man with a house near Embassy Row couldn't be trying *too* hard to hide.

"Yes, yes," Nathalie repeated. "We must be very chic."

I made a mental trip through my wardrobe and groaned. "I don't think. . . ."

But Nathalie wasn't listening. She was dragging me down the hallway to her bedroom, which I hadn't been invited to see before. It was almost completely mirrored and anything that wasn't a mirror was covered in red velvet. It was only two skips short of being a bordello. Those mistresses again, I wondered?

She flung open mirrored doors and began to root around in an enormous closet, pulling out dresses and flinging them around the room and across the bed and over the small upholstered chairs.

161

"What will it be? Oh, I'm so excited. The Ungaro that's way down on the hips? With a million strings of pearls and this big white hat? You like it?"

"Don't you think it's. . . ."

"What about this Yves Saint Laurent? It's the last thing Hallsey bought for me . . . you should have heard him moan. Millions for himself, but not one cent for me. You like it? I adore the melon with these crystal beads, don't you?" There were two round spots of color in her cheeks—two spots of color I had seen only once before . . . the night she drank champagne from the same glass as Ronald Chunk, the real estate baron.

"I. . . ."

"Or what about this Dior. Don't you love the shoulders? Or this Givenchy . . . one shoulder. I do have nice shoulders, don't you think? Or what about this black and white Guy Laroche?"

I was stunned. Was this the girl I had thought so badly dressed?

"All these clothes . . . I never saw you . . . I mean, I didn't imagine. . . ." I ran out of words.

She laughed and her laughter was gay and unaffected. The little lines of petulance habitually around her mouth had disappeared for the moment.

"You don't understand. I am a closet clothes horse. My men—they will never let me dress up. Always I must be the little girl. Hallsey fixed me permanently in time at approximately seventeen. *Toujours la jeune fille . . . zut!* With Martin it is a little better . . . he allows me to advance to approximately nineteen. With neither of them am I allowed to dress up and have a little fun and be a woman of the world. So I buy these beautiful clothes. And I try them on when I am alone. I dress up and prance around and smoke cigarettes from a long holder and practice walking with a slouch and a slink and dream of the time when I can do it all in public."

She began to pick up the dresses and hang them back in the closet.

"But surely, Nathalie, you could wear one of these. There must be something in that closet that would be appropriate."

She shook her head. "No. Not one. They won't do. Martin would be furious." The little lines of discontent were back around her mouth. "It will be the same all-enveloping caftan . . . it's the best I can do."

"Don't be absurd. Wear what you like. I'm sure Martin would approve." It didn't make sense. Why would two men buy her couturier clothes and then forbid her to wear them? Why would she have to fly to Paris for something suitable for her portrait?

She pulled open the doors to a second closet. It stood opposite a great full-length mirror and it was as crowded with gowns and hats and shoes as the first.

"These are from Rome. We made a flying trip there just for the fashions. I wanted to have my pick before they were shown in Paris. Valentino—you like it? This one I love with the dropped waistline. It's by Laug. Do you suppose a hat will be all right for six o'clock? No, no . . . Marcel would never allow it, even though he bought it for me."

We? Rome? That must have been Hallsey. A hat Martin had bought? And she was afraid to wear it?

"Try the Valentino, Nathalie. Let me decide."

She climbed into it, stripping to the buff in front of me without the least concern for modesty. The dress was white silk, low cut in front with cap sleeves and large black, yellow, red, and blue blossoms scattered artfully here and there.

A magnificent bit of dressmaking, one I would have given anything to own. But as she patted it into place over ample hips and pranced around the room I began to understand about the husbands. A strange transformation had taken place . . . the parlormaid had stepped into the queen's robes for a day and the parlormaid had never looked more

163

like a parlormaid. Nathalie was too young, too plump, and too ordinary for these extraordinary creations. She couldn't pull it off.

And something else . . . something that made no sense.

"Then why do they buy you all these expensive clothes if they won't allow you to wear them?" I could see now why they preferred not to let her prance around in these gowns—the strut and hip wriggling were absurd. But why buy them in the first place?

"Because, that's why." She stuck out an ample hip and pretended to puff on a long cigarette, chin in air, posing like a child trying to imitate a film star. "They know very well that I'll buy them myself if they don't, that's why."

Surely an empty threat. Each of these dresses cost thousands of dollars. "How?"

"Earn them."

"You're serious?"

"Oh, yes. Dewy youth and a French accent pay big money. And I always demanded a bonus—a trip to the couturier, you see. I always wore the very best. I worked only the highest priced hotels . . . the Ritz . . . the Plaza Athénée . . . the George V. Sometimes I went to London. I love the Connaught. All those lovely old men. I sit in the lounge with a Perrier. And presently one of them sidles up. 'Do you mind if I sit down?' Lustful old men, full of forbidden appetites, dreaming that this perfectly dressed young girl who has stirred their libidinous desires will somehow restore lost powers. And when they can't . . . oh, they are so pathetic then . . . it is a simple matter to ask for whatever one wants. Of course Marcel is different . . . he is young. But even he . . . from time to time. . . ."

She didn't finish She didn't have to. I understood.

No wonder her men refused to allow her to wear clothes that brought back her former profession. No wonder, further, that she didn't really fit them. Although, as I thought about it, a high-priced call girl didn't necessarily betray her career by looking out of place in fine clothes. There

164

had been a girl at the Heart Ball in the Bahamas, I remembered, who far outshone anyone present in both chic and beauty—and she had turned out to be an octoroon whose profession was marrying and divorcing wealthy men.

But Nathalie—Nathalie was something else, a simple, lazy girl who probably didn't even understand the implications of living as she had lived and preferred marriage simply because it was easier, though boring.

"Ah well," I sighed. "Perhaps the caftan, after all."

"Perhaps." She stripped off the Valentino and put it back on its hanger with loving care. "Perhaps not even that. A simple skirt and blouse, I think."

"I think, too. Actually, you are most charming like that." It was true.

"But so boring." She hung the dress back on the rod with a dissatisfied snap.

"Tonight will be different."

She brightened. "I hope so."

"There will be interesting people to meet. You said so yourself." I wanted to cheer her up. I felt sorry for her. She was a child whose candy had been snatched away.

"It will be fun, won't it? Do you think it will be fun, Persis? We never go anywhere. And Marcel won't even let me have a part in his movies, although I know I can act and I'm not afraid of nude scenes."

I'll bet, I thought. But he wouldn't put her in a pornographic film. She was posing as his wife, after all. Suppose somebody recognized her?

"Never mind about Marcel's movies. Tonight will be exciting. You will meet new friends and you will be invited everywhere and you'll never be bored in Marseille again."

"Exciting. Yes, that's what I'd like. An exciting evening. Hurry and dress, Persis, and let's go. I've been longing for something exciting to happen."

As I dressed, I hoped she wouldn't be disappointed.

165

Thirty-Four

Nathalie was right—the street Von Berger lived on was elegant. Great plane trees cast luxurious shadows. Fine white Mediterranean houses peered out at us from behind wrought-iron gates. Even the exuberant Marseille traffic was subdued in passing, out of respect for wealth and power.

Nathalie was driving and she pulled up at the address Von Berger had indicated with a flourish and a squealing of brakes. "Driving is one of my sports," she had said earlier, and I believed her. On the way over she had given as good as she got from the other French drivers and had come out, I thought, just a shade the better of even the most daring. The chariot races in Nero's Rome couldn't have stirred the blood more than her careening progress across the teeming city had stirred mine. Our breathless arrival in one piece at Von Berger's gate convinced me that there was still a God in His heaven and I sighed with relief at the prospect of descending from Nathalie's infernal machine and relaxing in Von Berger's fine house.

But it was not to be.

A servant greeted us at the gate with new instructions. We were not, it appeared, to be allowed to alight. Von Berger had encountered difficulties with his schedule and would not be back in Marseille in time to entertain us here. Would we mind terribly meeting him at a rendezvous outside the city? He would be sure to get that far and the distance for us would not be an imposition. Naturally, since we were being so disagreeably inconvenienced, he would expect us to dine with him as well. Martin had been informed and would be present. The restaurant, La Bonne Auberge, was one of the finest on the Côte d'Azur. He promised it.

"La Bonne Auberge. I thought it was just beyond Antibes. That's not close." I remembered vaguely that I had dined there once long ago.

"I've heard of it, too. But it must be where he says it is. We can be there in thirty minutes. Twenty, if I put my mind to it."

"No please. Let's take our time." I was still disturbed and I tried to root around in my memory to fix La Bonne Auberge firmly in a geographic space. But it had been long ago. And furthermore, France was covered with places called La Bonne Auberge, just as it is covered with places called Villefranche and Le Mas and Le Moulin and L'Oasis and a million other things that come out in quadruplicate or worse throughout the country. The French have a theory that if you find a good thing you stick with it. So, now that I think of it, does everyone else.

Still, the unease persisted. "Nathalie, do you think we should? It's a long drive. And it will be dark."

She laughed. "Don't be silly, Persis. I'm a fabulous driver and it will be fun. And anyway, we have to go— Marcel is undoubtedly already on his way."

So the die was cast.

She wheeled the Peugeot around and we were off, Nathalie doing battle with the traffic while I deciphered the directions the servant had supplied in writing.

"I can't make too much of this map," I apologized, squinting.

"Naturally. That man was an Algerian."

"An Algerian? How did you know?"

"You can't miss the type. There are millions of them in Marseille. They'll do anything to make a franc. I must say that I'm surprised: you'd think Von Berger could find someone a little better than that to work for him."

167

But then we both forgot about it. After all, he was only a gatekeeper so what could one expect?

Nathalie hurtled across the city, the Peugeot screaming in and out among the columns of traffic like a demented greyhound. We streaked past apartment buildings and soccer fields and commercial areas and camping grounds standing barren and lonely as they waited for the onslaught of summer. The kilometers flew by and Nathalie laughed aloud whenever she overtook a car and roared past it, clinging to the outer lane until the last possible moment before an approaching vehicle forced her back in line.

Now she began to sing in a high but piercing voice that carried clearly over the noise of the traffic around us.

"Milord," she crooned—that great lament-invitation of Edith Piaf. And I translated mentally as she sang. "Come on, mister, sit at my table and make yourself comfortable. Tell me your troubles and put your feet up on a chair. I know you, though you've never seen me. I'm only a tramp, a phantom of the street. . . ."

The notes were high and clear, but they were not the notes of Piaf. Nathalie may have lived a little of the chanteuse's early life, but that was the only similarity. The heart was missing.

She switched without a pause to Jo Dassin's "Allez Roulez," a song more suited to her style and she whipped through it with energy and verve.

Then it was back to Piaf. This time I joined her and the two of us sang at the tops of our lungs, vying with one another for the highest note and the longest held.

"Non, je ne regrette rien . . . nothing that's been done to me, good or ill. Everything's paid for, swept up, forgotten. I don't give a damn for the past . . . I'm starting at zero again. My life, my happiness, begins with you."

It sounded better in French, of course, and that's how we sang it . . . our voices trembling, Piaf style, and each of us thinking of someone. At least I suppose we were . . . I know I was thinking of Dana and feeling bereft and

168

cheated and sad, just as Piaf intended. I don't know whether Nathalie was thinking of Martin or Bryce or if, indeed, she was thinking of anyone at all. Probably not. It is possible that she was just singing.

In any case, the caterwauling—and I'm afraid that's exactly what it was—made the kilometers fly. And by the time we had gone through "Le Chanteur des Rues," "Pauvre Pierrot," "Bye, Bye Louis," "Je Suis à Toi," "Les Mots d'Amour," and several others (repeating each one several times to perfect our performance) we had arrived at the *carrefour* where La Bonne Auberge was supposed to be found.

But there was nothing there. There was a crossroads, but there was nothing on it except a few rusty road signs to Nice, to Cannes, and—as always—to Paris.

We re-studied the map, both of us poring over it at the side of the road. There was no question—we were at the right crossroads. But where was the Auberge?

"We haven't made a mistake." Nathalie was puzzled but firm about that. "So it must be Von Berger who has erred."

"We'll have to ask. It's getting late."

"Such stupidity! And he's so good looking. Who would ever suspect?" She threw the car into gear and we were off, searching for a farmhouse.

They weren't hard to find. In fact we found three before anyone could do more than stare at us when we asked for the vanished restaurant.

The fourth farmer was articulate, but not very helpful. "No such thing around here, and I was born on this place. No Bonne Auberge, I assure you. Maybe in Antibes or Cap Ferrat or St. Tropez—that's where you find the good eating places . . . that's where the money is. Film stars, millionaires. If you're looking for good cuisine, that's where you'll find it."

Antibes. I knew I'd been there. But Antibes was too long

169

a drive. Von Berger would never have expected us to meet him there.

I didn't like it. I hadn't liked it since the Algerian turned us away from his gate, refusing to let us turn into the drive.

The farmer went back inside and Nathalie and I sat in the car and stared at one another.

"What now?" She looked on the brink of tears with frustration and disappointment. Furthermore, we were beginning to be hungry. It had been a long time since lunch at Arles.

"I don't know. Let's think." But there was something else on my mind. "Did you notice the house?" It hadn't registered at the time but now a picture of it was materializing clearly in my mind.

"What house?" Houses bored her: she was solely concerned with restaurants.

"Von Berger's."

"I didn't see it. We never went in, remember?" Crossly, regretting it. Thinking I was crazy to be thinking about Von Berger's house when we couldn't even find Von Berger.

"I looked at it. Just a quick glimpse. And it didn't register at first."

"Well, what about it?"

"I'm not positive—but I had this strange impression."

She was impatient. That was the past: what she wanted to know was what to do with the present. "So?"

"I think it was empty." I'd said it and as I spoke I realized I didn't just think it—I was sure. It was one of those quick images that don't mature until later.

We were both silent, each of us considering the implications. Finally she spoke.

"What does it mean?"

"I don't know. Why would he ask us there if it was empty?"

"Maybe it was scheduled to be a housewarming. Maybe the furniture will come later."

"Maybe."

"Maybe everybody was supposed to bring something for the house and he forgot to tell us."

"It could be."

"And maybe everybody he invited will be waiting for us at the restaurant when we get there."

"Nathalie, there isn't any restaurant."

"I don't believe you." Her voice trembled and she spoke very loud to convince herself.

"I'm afraid it's true. There isn't any restaurant."

"But there *must* be. We have only to go on looking. One farmer doesn't know everything."

"We have looked. And it's getting dark."

"Well, I don't believe you. He wouldn't give us a map and everything if there wasn't a restaurant. I'm going to go on looking. It's a known fact that Algerians can't read and write and they certainly can't be expected to draw maps people can follow."

"That Algerian could write. La Bonne Auberge was lettered as clearly as anyone could have lettered."

"Never mind. It was an Algerian. So the restaurant could be right around the corner. And you only imagined that the house was empty—I didn't notice it. And I'm not going to miss a good time just because we can't read a map correctly."

She had made a decision. The car roared forward, spitting dirt behind it. In the hen house chickens woke up and cried out in alarm and a dog inside the barn began a deep-throated protest.

I shrugged and settled down in my seat. There was nothing else to do.

She was a tenacious searcher. We explored every road, poked into every cart track. We crossed and criss-crossed every intersection no matter how insignificant. We stopped and queried a half-dozen people. It grew dark. And still no Bonne Auberge.

Finally she surrendered. "We might as well go home and have something to eat. I'm exhausted and starved."

171

I was relieved. I didn't like what was going on and I didn't like Von Berger. The only reason I had consented to come was to learn what I could about why he was in Marseille and to try to find out if he was aware of the Praha show. As for me, my excuse for being in Marseille would be that I had read about Praha's exhibition and come especially on behalf of the gallery. No one could quarrel with that. And now here we were, in the country miles from Boulevard Longchamp—hungry, out of sorts, and wondering what had become of our much-anticipated evening.

We were too disappointed and dispirited to note the dim headlights at first. It wasn't until we had driven several miles that I became aware of them. Nathalie was too busy clinging to the winding road. I thought it odd that, despite the dark, they didn't use their brights. I turned in my seat to watch. They never came closer. They didn't drop back.

Suddenly the brights came on, and the vehicle speeded up until it was only a couple of car lengths behind us.

"My God!" Nathalie flung one arm up in front of her face, blinded. I reached in front of her and steadied the wheel. With the other hand I switched the rear-view mirror from light to eye-protecting dark. Nathalie's grip on the wheel tightened. "It's all right. I've got it."

"They must want to pass. Can you pull over a little?"

"Bastards. Why should I?" She was a combatant, not a driver.

"Because he'll blind you, that's why."

"Never! Pray to the Virgin." And she stayed where she was. So did the other car.

I protested again. No use: she had the bit in her teeth. So I settled down in my seat. It was the only thing I could do.

We went on like that. Nathalie stuck to her speed and so did the car behind, never varying its distance. In the brilliant light that bathed our front seat I could see the girl's lower lip jutting out in anger and determination.

Mile after mile. If we increased our speed, so did they. If we decelerated, they did too.

They didn't drop back. They didn't try to pass.

I was beginning to twist my fingers together to keep from speaking.

It was Nathalie who spoke first. "Bastards. Fresh kids. Playing chicken. Trying to scare us. Well, they won't scare me."

And she stayed her course. Once in a while she tried to lose them, but the Peugeot wasn't equal to the task. Once in a while she slowed suddenly. But they were expert drivers or else they could read her mind, because when she slowed suddenly so did they.

Finally we came to a straight stretch of road and we could see the lights of Marseille in the distance.

"Almost home." I had never seen a more welcome sight. I didn't believe they were pranksters—not after this evening's itinerary. But I didn't want to frighten the girl. What good would it do? And now—so near the city—surely we were safe.

"Finally," Nathalie answered through tightly clenched teeth. "And you can bet I'll complain to the first '*flic*' I see. Note the license number if you can, Persis."

She put her foot down on the gas and the Peugeot responded like a game pony, giving us all it had. But it wasn't enough. At that same moment, our pursuer shot forward, engulfing us in light. The girl was screaming at her Peugeot, calling on it for more speed, shrieking orders, exhorting and commanding.

"Nathalie—let them pass. Are you mad?"

But she wouldn't. And her Peugeot struggled with all its heart to obey.

But the pursuer was upon us. We drowned in the bright lights. Then it was abreast of us and careening along beside us. We were a team, charging at breakneck speed. Bright orange bursts came from the left. And then they were past, rocketing away from us into the night.

173

The Peugeot slowed. The Peugeot stopped.

There was absolute quiet.

We stared ahead, neither of us willing to say the unsayable.

But somebody had to.

"Persis?" I could scarcely hear her. It was only a whisper in the night.

"I know."

"Is it true?"

"I think so. Yes."

"But it couldn't be."

We were quiet again, thinking about that.

Finally. "You saw?"

"I did."

"You're sure?"

"I'm afraid so."

"Did you see faces?"

"No. Did you?"

"No."

I could feel her shaking beside me. "You mustn't. We're all right. We have to get home, Nathalie. Don't go to pieces."

"I know. I can't help it."

"I'll drive."

"Please."

We changed places. She slipped over and I was the one who walked around the car and got into the driver's seat because I was, as it turned out, the stronger.

The Peugeot started up obediently.

The small voice beside me had only two questions as we crept quietly into Marseille.

"You saw it, Persis?"

"I did."

"They were shooting at us?"

"Yes, Nathalie." There wasn't any question.

Then why hadn't they killed us? Everyone else was being killed. Why wait so long to shoot at us? Why wait until

174

we were almost back in Marseille? It didn't make sense. Was I going mad?

Martin was not there when we finally reached number eighteen, Boulevard Longchamp; but Nathalie wasn't alarmed. He had not, it seemed, ever attempted to rendezvous with Von Berger. The day's shooting had not gone well and everyone was working overtime in order to stay on schedule. There was a note from the maid saying that he would not be home until well after midnight.

Nathalie and I rummaged in the refrigerator for leftovers and thanked heaven he wasn't wandering around, like us, somewhere in the hinterlands searching for the nonexistent Bonne Auberge and being shot at by strangers in the night.

We toasted our safe return with a nightcap of Porto and fell into our respective beds, exhausted.

I didn't even stay awake long enough to admire the floodlit Virgin from my bedroom window. Which wasn't very grateful: maybe, after all, it was her gracious beneficence that had delivered Nathalie and me. Nothing would have surprised me that night.

▥ *Thirty-Five*

I slept late the next morning and even so woke up exhausted. Nothing drains one's energy like a dark night, a fast chase, and a few bullets. My whole body hurt as much as if I had been in an automobile accident.

Well, I almost had.

Nathalie and Martin were not in evidence when I pulled

175

myself together and staggered off to the museum around noon. And after that I was too busy to worry about anything except Praha and frames and installation and whether or not the Press would continue to cover the story as expertly as it had to date.

The young curators were as disorganized as ever while being at the same time as insoucient as ever. It was a perfect example of organized chaos.

Somehow I found the time to check on Von Berger's house by calling *La Marseillaise*. The foreign desk helped me out. I didn't even have to invent a story. All I said was I'd been invited to a party at a house near the Turkish embassy and no one was there. He asked for the address. I told him. In two minutes he was back to inform me that I must have had the wrong number—the owners of the house I'd gone to were diplomats currently posted to Djibouti. The house was empty, unfurnished, and for let.

I didn't ask about Von Berger. I thought I knew all I needed to know about him.

When I returned around six, Nathalie greeted me.

"Don't say anything to Marcel about last night." The two bright spots were back in her cheeks.

"But why not?"

"Because *I* haven't. After I got home I realized that last night was the most excitement I'd had since I got here. And if we tell Marcel he'll never let me go anywhere again. Imagine—the first time I'm out in Marseille without him and we get shot at. It's pretty wonderful when you think about it."

"It's wonderful that we weren't hurt."

"Even the car wasn't hurt. There isn't a mark on it. They were just trying to scare us. Well, I wasn't scared."

"I was."

"Oh, Persis, don't be an old woman. Nobody was hurt. I don't believe they intended to hurt us or they would have."

I wasn't so sure. "Maybe."

"In any case, be that as it may, don't tell Marcel. I am asking you—begging you."

How could I refuse. "All right."

"Promise?"

Reluctantly, because I believed it was wrong and that he should be told, I promised.

She clapped her hands. "You're a good sport. And you've made me very happy."

"It isn't fair to him, you know."

"Don't be silly. He's like Hallsey—always thinking about money. Only Hallsey has tons more—never mind about how he gets it—and Marcel has to scramble for his. I thought he was so rich. But he has to keep scratching. He likes to live like a king—big houses, yachts. But believe me, he earns every cent of it himself."

She sighed. Evidently she was disillusioned about the amount of his income.

"I like a man who works for his money," I said.

"Depends. Depends on how hard he has to scratch to get it."

And with that final word she went off to dress for dinner.

▥ *Thirty-Six*

Dinner that night was from a menu selected by Martin; and it was so grand luxe I wondered if it was supposed to be a Last Supper. We began with champagne and proceeded to a series of glorious wines accompanying an hors d'oeuvres of *truffe en croûte*, a fish course of *filet de bar à la julienne des légumes*, an entrée of *noix de ris de veau aux champig-*

177

nons sauvages (the mushrooms, so Martin informed me, flown in from the forests of Fontainbleau), a *plateau de fromages* and *les délices de Marjorie*. Marjorie was the cook and the *'délices'* were her sinful miniature fruit tarts.

Nathalie ate with unbridled enthusiasm; Martin with restrained dignity. I scarcely touched anything that passed before me: it was a matter of nerves.

"You 'guard the line'?" Martin asked after watching me push the food around plate after plate while scarcely sampling anything.

"Oui—je garde la ligne. Je m'excuse, Marcel."

Nathalie, happy as a cat in cream, couldn't understand. "But it's so good, Persis. Why come to France, if not to eat?"

"Why, indeed?" The look Martin gave me was full of cynicism and inquiry.

"And anyway, you're thinner than I am by far. But remember, men don't like to go to bed with a skeleton . . . just bear that in mind."

Martin laughed and without comment lit his usual after-dinner cigar. The room was engulfed in smoke.

Also as usual, Nathalie coughed. "Marcel—you know I can't stand your cigars. I can't breathe."

He laughed again. "What I know is that you're longing to leave us and watch television. Always looking for adventure. What is it tonight?"

She was already on her feet: it was the evening ritual. "It's 'Dallas,' Marcel. Do come and watch. J.R. is just about to. . . ."

Martin waved her out of the room. "Run along. Persis and I will finish our coffee here and then join you."

She rushed out of the dining room and clattered down the hall. In a second we heard the sound of the music that heralded the beginning of her program.

He poured me a brandy and offered me a cheroot, which I politely declined, and we sat in companionable silence. He was very small and very compact and very neatly put

178

together and I looked at him and thought about how much I needed someone I could trust. Everything was piling up on me.

He sat there like a perfect little miniature of a man, wearing a black velvet smoking jacket, rather warm, I thought, for this evening. His small feet were snugly encased in velvet slippers with his initials embroidered in gold. There was a gold bracelet on his right wrist and an impossibly thin Piaget gold watch on his left. The gold and black made a sharp contrast with his fawn-colored shirt and flannel trousers.

A perfect little dandy, I thought. Too perfect, maybe.

And then I thought, things have arrived at a critical point.

I must have someone to trust. Dana has vanished and Blessing hasn't appeared.

But was that someone Martin? Was he a man to be trusted?

I studied him, trying to disguise the intensity of my regard by watching through lowered lashes.

Somebody was trying to kill me. Hadn't there been a car pursuing us? Hadn't I been shot at—for the second time?

But was Martin to be trusted?

Well, I had to trust somebody, didn't I? I couldn't go on alone forever. And Martin had already helped me, after all.

"Could we close the door? I would like to speak to you."

And I told him. Not a word about last night. But everything else.

Everything.

179

Thirty-Seven

Martin went out later that evening, saying he had a camera crew filming night scenes down at the Old Port. Nathalie begged to go with him. She said she never had any excitement. It seemed to me that between Nathalie and the young museum director someone was always complaining about the lack of excitement in Marseille; whereas I, for my part, found it quite exciting enough.

He explained to her patiently that he couldn't take her because it was a dangerous area. He'd be too busy to keep an eye on her, and he'd be worrying about her when he should be concentrating on his work. Further, it would be very late when he returned.

In fact, he never returned.

Nathalie had wanted excitement, and she got it. The police found Martin's body late the next afternoon. He was slumped over a picnic table at a parking stop on the autoroute outside the city. All day long people passing had thought he was a traveler taking a nap, until finally someone noticed the small black hole in the back of his head.

The police were not unduly upset. Death was as ordinary an event in Marseille as the ritual coffee or whiskey taken at the corner tabac before going off to work in the morning. People were murdered every day. For example, they pointed out, yesterday they had found the bodies of two men executed in the same fashion.

They had both been mercenary soldiers.

Thirty-Eight

Somehow—I don't know how—we got through it.

Nathalie had him buried immediately.

"I want it over," she said.

She was convinced that it was her fault. Bryce, she was certain, had ordered his execution. But Bryce was nowhere evident. Neither was anyone else we knew from home.

I was equally certain that it was my fault. After all, hadn't I involved him in the Lassiter affair and wasn't such involvement turning out to be a death sentence for everyone?

Like Lassiter and the six other dead Englishmen, he'd made inquiries in the wrong places. Now, like them, and like the two mercenaries we'd interviewed, he was very much dead.

It was the dreariest of funerals. Naturally, it rained. There weren't many of us. His film crew and a few unimpressive-looking actors. The museum staff, who had come as a courtesy to me. We huddled under our black umbrellas like a collection of mournful crows, noses dripping with a combination of tears and raindrops, and shoes squishing wretchedly in the wet grass.

Then, as suddenly as it had happened, it was over.

Martin was gone. The film people were gone. The museum staff was pursuing their business.

Nathalie shut herself in her bedroom for about half an hour and then settled down to await the arrival of Hallsey Bryce: I was sure she had been in touch with him and was

181

expecting him momentarily. Nathalie was a girl who had no intention of living without a man—as long as he bought her clothes.

Marcel Martin had suffered an unfortunate accident. He was gone. She would move back to her first protector. Life was like that. A girl had to look after herself. And maybe her sojourn with Martin had taught the tight-fisted Hallsey a lesson. Who could tell?

What would become of her? I didn't know, and I didn't have to worry about it, because she was a survivor. I would not abandon her. I would be at her side until help arrived. But there was another very pressing concern.

Because suddenly it was Friday, the day of the dress rehearsal.

▥ *Thirty-Nine*

The opera house was wreathed in quiet, its six Ionic columns the epitomy of unruffled dignity. Its frieze of classic figures gazed down at passers-by with monumental calm.

Anyone who knew anything about theater would know that the great house was holding its breath, waiting for the hour of dress to arrive.

The stage was silent. The fly floor was abandoned. The orchestra stalls were empty. The instruments were covered.

In an hour the scene would turn into chaos. But now the house slept.

I had come well in advance and stationed the car at the

side of the small *Place* where I would have a clear view of anyone coming or going.

I saw the director cross the *Place* and approach the doors. She was very dignified today in a dark silk dress and white plastic earrings. A doorman let her in, ogling her slim, silk-sheathed body.

I had chosen a spot where my car would not stand out: others were moving about, arriving and departing. I ignored them and concentrated on the opera house.

Fifteen minutes passed. Another fifteen. Then two black Mercedes slid up and parked as close as possible to the entrance. Three men leapt from the first car and scanned the area. They were young, athletic, wearing dark glasses and three piece suits, neatly fitted.

They bounded up the steps to the main door and wrapped a smart tattoo. I saw the director let them in.

A minute or two passed during which I assumed they had checked out the lobby, giving cursory attention to the scattered pieces of sculpture and checking the curved marble staircases on either side.

After a short time they emerged and nodded to the occupants of the second Mercedes. They opened the doors to the first car. Simultaneously a group of men leapt from the second automobile, surrounding someone who emerged from car number one, completely hiding the occupant from view.

Woman? Man? I couldn't tell.

All I could make out was a block of bodies in dark clothes. There was just no way anyone could have penetrated that tight-knit unit. Together, in a block, they swept into the building.

I counted to ninety. I thought it would give them the right amount of time. Then I was across the street and up the steps and knocking at the door. The director opened it. She gasped when she saw me.

I didn't blame her. I had seen enough of Marseille to know that there was just one kind of female who did not

183

wear skirts—the delivery girls who carried messages and packages around the city. No one ever really looked at them: they affected a sexless image deliberately designed to put off the most amorous of males and to assure their getting in and out of offices in one piece.

Today I was one of those. I had taken my jeans and shirt to the park and rolled them in the dust. I had rented a pair of motorcycle boots and a white helmet from the boy who served juice at the *buvette* in the park. I carried a blue musette bag on which I had lettered UNISEX COIFFEUSE, HAIRDRESSERS TO THE STARS. It was very professional. The bag was filled with hairdressing equipment. It was my one chance to get inside the opera house.

"Delivery. Unisex Coiffeuse," I said.

The director was stunned.

"M. . . ."

I rushed to interrupt her, to stop her from saying my name, "I was told to deliver this hairdressing equipment before seven. I was told someone would be here to receive it."

"Ah, yes," she said, gathering her wits.

"So here it is—if you'll sign?" My eyes were moving around the room. Six men were watching. They had quick eyes and bunched muscles and they hadn't made up their minds yet what to do about me. I would have another moment or two to try to decide which of them was the important one before I had to leave.

And there was someone else. A woman. She was crossing the room, coming directly toward me. Disaster marching my way.

"Persis Willum," she was saying. "What a surprise. What are you doing in that ridiculous get-up?"

It was Kate Cochran. And she wasn't smiling.

184

🎞 *Forty*

She did it so smoothly that I doubt the director had any inkling of what was happening. First she linked her arm in mine; then one of the men swung in on my other side, and with astonishing speed we were out the door and in the back seat of the Mercedes with Cochran flinging a "thank you" and "the money will be deposited to the museum account" over her shoulder as we went. The rest of the party followed with equal speed and the two cars took off. I had not said a word. And with good reason—there was a gun pressed firmly to my back. I doubt if the director saw that, either.

When we were under way Cochran finally spoke to me.

"I'm sorry it's you, Persis. I've always liked you."

I chose not to examine the implications of that remark. "How," I asked instead, "did you find out about the exhibition?"

She laughed. "I clip newspapers—remember? *The New York Times* ran a story, among others."

The two cars were racing out of Marseille, weaving effortlessly in and out of traffic. The men did not speak. Looking at them and noting their bunched muscles and shifting eyes I understood them for what they were—thugs, Marseille brand. I could see bulges in their tight-fitting suits that meant every one of them was armed.

We were on the outskirts of Marseille before Cochran

spoke again. "It's a shame about your being there, Persis."

I tried, although I didn't expect much. "I was there just by chance."

"In that costume?" She laughed again. It was not the kind of laugh that made you want to smile back. "No. And I'm sorry, truly sorry. But you pose a problem and it will have to be dealt with. But not by me." She did not speak again.

We had left the city behind and were winding our way swiftly along the edge of the sea. The terrain was getting rougher, more wooded. Houses were thinning out. So was the traffic: we flew past only an occasional "Deux Chevaux." The countryside became increasingly wild and unkempt.

We began to climb. There were no other cars now.

The surroundings became frankly hostile. We left the main road and turned onto a smaller one and after a few kilometers we left that one, too, and bumped onto an even more primitive trail, the Mercedes's springs suffering in martyred silence. To occupy my mind I tried to memorize our route, but it was hopeless . . . there seemed to be endless small trails overlapping one another in the piny woods and I had the impression that we were taking them all.

Suddenly we were plunging downward. I was sure that we had reached and passed the crest of the Corniche. Abruptly we began to climb again, still hurtling along at surprising speed. Up and down—a roller-coaster ride to . . . what?

When the wall appeared in front of us it was a total surprise.

There was no approach. We simply burst out of the woods like a bullet and there it was in a rough clearing, a high wall with an iron gate and roofs just visible inside the compound. There was a frantic barking of dogs—large dogs. The quiet sound of our motors had nevertheless put them into full cry. Yet the place had a tranquil appearance, like a typical south-of-France *mas*—walled properties are not unusual among well-to-do landowners in France. There was really nothing to suggest that this was an armed fortress.

So when two armed men suddenly appeared and looked into both cars, even examining the uninteresting contents of my hairdressing bag, I was surprised. I shouldn't have been, but I was.

The examination was swift but thorough. Then we were motioned through the gate.

"Don't make trouble, Persis," Cochran said. "Just cooperate."

"With whom?" I hoped that I didn't sound as frightened as I felt; but the gun was digging into my side and it didn't inspire confidence.

I knew that we were on our way to meet the man who had been the cause of everything that had happened. In seconds now I would meet him face to face. It was for this that I had arranged the Praha exhibition. For this I had exposed myself in the opera house lobby. Everything had been for this . . .

Cochran was the unexpected particular, the detail that didn't compute.

But the man himself? I had a mental image, carefully assembled since the assassination of Lassiter and, scared though I was, I couldn't resist a small surge of excitement at the prospect of finally meeting him.

What would he be like? He would be a man of between sixty and seventy years of age—maybe even as young as fifty-five. He would be a recluse, not wanting to draw attention. He might be a man of many names, with a taste for the good things in life, even if he could only enjoy them in private. He would like expensive wines, food, art, women . . . why else would he rob and kill? He would be arrogant, cruel, ruthless, and amoral. He might even still be attractive to women—as certainly he had once been.

A sculptor's assistant, Cochran had said, so he would know a good deal about art.

187

A murderer. A killer. A man I was about to meet.

"Cooperate with whom?" I repeated.

"You will see in a moment. I suppose you read the same article I did and came rushing over here to see what it was all about?"

"Not exactly. I don't have your kind of income."

We were out of the car now and being escorted across a small courtyard and through the French doors of the foyer. Inside, the floors were parquet, the walls hung with what looked to me like medieval tapestries. At the head of the stairway that wound upward to the left was a large Rubens nude. We turned right and proceeded down a corridor lined with African masks. Whoever my host was, his tastes were eclectic.

We paused before a heavy chased bronze door. It must have come from some Italian Renaissance church—spoils of war in a long-forgotten French adventure abroad. One of our escorts knocked.

"Open up," Cochran called impatiently. "We have a problem."

The door opened with surprising suddenness, operated by some device at the fingertips of the man who sat behind the vast mahogany Chippendale desk at the far end of the room.

"The photographs?" His voice was harsh, his face in shadow.

"The photographs were all right. There was nothing. *She* is the problem . . . Persis Willum. She's smart. She's here. But why? She's in the middle of everything. What does she have to do with it? We must know."

Even in the poor light, even with the light behind him I recognized him as the man I'd seen twice in Praha's photos—Praha didn't need artificial lighting to get an accurate impression, even at night.

"You know my name; but I don't know yours." Daylight was fading fast. Cochran switched on a light. "You are . . . ?"

188

"Zed—just call me Zed. It won't matter."

I looked quickly around the room. Computers. Several TV screens. An assortment of paintings of the French school. A framed certificate from the city of Marseille—something about "invaluable service in wartime." A small statuette of the Virgin that guards the Old Port standing on the corner of his desk . . . I'd seen a million like it in the tourist traps that line the waterfront, but this one was different—it was gold.

"The statue is a memento?"

Cochran couldn't resist. "He is a hero of the city of Marseille. He saved the Virgin during the war."

That was it. Things began to fall in place with the precision of mail dropping through the slot in the front door of Gregor's gallery in Gull Harbor. A murderer who had been a sculptor's assistant and understood casts and molds and metals, who understood handling statues on any scale. A massacre on a beach during which a shipment of gold had vanished and after which dead bodies in bits and pieces of German uniform were found. The subsequent betrayal of the petty criminals of the Old Port, their round-up and execution. Zed—savior of the Virgin. The gold reproduction on his desk.

Of course.

My throat closed with excitement. Nonetheless, I could speak and the words came in a rush.

"And I know how he saved the city. I can tell you. Stop me if I'm wrong."

I didn't give them a chance to stop me. "He knew all about casting on a heroic scale. He had been a sculptor's assistant, probably a sculptor who did heroic figures for monuments and memorials. That was in the beginning. The Allies were bombing the harbor during the war; the city fathers were terrified for the safety of the city's greatest treasure—the gilded Virgin. This man—Zed, as he calls himself—went to them and said 'I can save your Virgin. I will erect a substitute until the danger is over.' "

189

I was too excited now to worry about Zed or anything else because the puzzle was unraveling itself perfectly.

"As I said, he had been a sculptor's assistant. He knew his stuff. He made molds of the original Virgin and he and his men substituted a Virgin made of solid gold—Czechoslovakian gold. There was no danger—he knew from the Englishmen he worked with that the Allies had agreed among themselves to spare the monument."

The man in the window hadn't moved. Cochran seemed stunned. "Gold? What gold?"

"Gold the British were trying to save for the Czechs. Zed was part of a team trying to get it out of France. There was a rendezvous set up with a British cruiser. The cruiser never arrived, probably its disappearance can be attributed to Zed. Anyway, he hired mercenaries, put them in German uniforms as a cover, massacred his own people, took off with the gold, and then betrayed his mercenaries to the Germans, who dispatched them. After the war he simply restored the original Virgin, melted down the false Virgin, and shipped the gold off to Swiss banks."

All these days I'd been staring at the Virgin in the harbor—climbing up inside her, studying her construction, admiring her golden glitter—but not until I saw the miniature of her in solid gold did it all fall into place.

"That, too?" Cochran said. She had been standing behind me. Now she stepped up beside me. We three were the only people in the room—our escort had left. "And Martin," she demanded, "what about Martin? The news came over the press wire that he was dead. Your handiwork?" She was addressing Zed, her voice tight with anger. He did not bother to respond, and she went on, with mounting fury. "Yes, I suppose it was. He got in your way somehow. Too many questions? And Nadia Milonsky—did you have to have her murdered? All I asked you to do was to get the book back and destroy it. But murder—you didn't have to do that. Lassiter, too. You're a monster.

190

You kill for pleasure.'' She was actually shaking with fury from head to foot.

"Never for pleasure," he said virtuously, the way you might say "I never touch cigarettes." "You are too emotional. You have always known what I am—I make no apologies. And it was your idea to come here to make certain about the photographs." The only emotion he betrayed was in taking two steps toward her. In doing so he stepped into the light from the lamp Cochran had turned on. I could see his face now and the sudden recognition hit me a hammer blow exactly between the eyes.

"I had to. You know I had to. If there had been anything. . . ." She didn't finish, but she threw me an anguished glance I couldn't interpret. And yet . . . and yet. . . .

"It's all I've done for thirty years. Combing newspapers for anything that would threaten. Covering up. Guarding. Trying to make sure." She had herself tightly in hand now. Her tone was controlled, dangerous.

"I would thank you, except that I know you don't do it out of love for me."

"Especially not out of love for you. You are garbage."

This time he reacted swiftly. He took another two steps toward her, and with the two of them standing face to face, I finally saw it. I saw three faces together in a collage of features.

"Von Berger." I didn't even realize I had spoken aloud.

They turned to me simultaneously, two animals surprised in battle and now at bay.

"Of course. How could I have been so stupid—and I'm supposed to be an artist. Your son. It must have happened while you were a student in Paris, Cochran. What did you do, farm the infant out? Of course you did. To impoverished German gentry, I suppose. And he doesn't know. You must have been frantic when he turned up in Gull Harbor after all those years of protecting him. If he found out his father was a murderer. . . ."

191

"It would kill him." She said it as a fact, almost with relief.

"You warned Zed that Lassiter was coming—might stumble onto something. And you also went to interview Milonsky and saw the book. . . ." I began to understand about Cochran.

The telephone rang. Zed picked it up. Cochran paid no attention. Neither did I. We were absorbed in each other.

"Quite by accident. I was nosing around during the interview. I spotted it hidden among her art books. But I wasn't able to take it—she never left me alone for a minute."

Nadia hadn't destroyed the book after all. She had kept it as a reminder of an earlier form of her genius and it had killed her.

"I always kept in touch with him." She gestured toward Zed, who was listening on the phone. "I'm not proud. But it was in both our interests that no one should know he was a murderer. All I can say to defend myself is that I was trying to protect my son." She sighed. "I wish you hadn't come, Persis. You know too much—knew too much from the beginning. I thought at the start that I could use you, but when you turned up in Marseille . . . If you gave your word, perhaps . . . ?"

"That won't be necessary." Zed had put down the phone. "It seems you were followed from the opera house—the Mitzu Brigade. Our information is that they're on their way—we expect an attack at any moment. They are confident they can persuade me to tell them where to find the gold." He smiled. The smile surprised me. It had charm. "We've been expecting something like this for a long time. We're ready—more than ready. They will have a surprise." He opened the desk drawer. "A terrorist attack is a useful conceit: people are killed during such events."

"No," Cochran cried. "No more killing."

He smiled again and this time I saw front teeth that

192

pushed into one another like the front teeth of a stable rat. "You needn't worry—she won't die alone."

"No. I won't allow it!"

"You've become a nuisance. Especially now that you know about the gold. And a danger. So very sorry." He did not look sorry; his eyes glittered and he was still smiling.

He brought the gun level.

Deliberate.

Unhurried.

Arm straight. Hand clenched.

Taking his time.

The gun steadied. With stunning speed Cochran threw the lamp at him. The room plunged into semidarkness.

Then came the sounds. The world reverberated and recoiled. There were five, six, seven great explosions. The sky lit up—the earth trembled. Bombs, I thought. They've crashed a truck through the main gate.

There was a pounding of gunfire in the compound.

Zed had recovered his balance. The gun swung in a small arc. I moved at the same instant and the bullet and I hit Cochran together. The weight of my body spun her sideways and she dropped. I heard him swear, saw the gleam of his shirtfront, registered the flicker of the ruby in his tie clasp. A fugitive bit of light hit the barrel of his gun: it was still pointed at Cochran. I felt in the bag slung over my shoulder for something—anything—to use as a weapon.

My fingers closed on a smoothness. I stepped up to Zed and struck at him. I heard the gun go off. I struck again. And this time he turned on me. I pressed the nozzle of the can in my hand and shot flood upon flood of hair spray into his unprotected eyes. He flailed with the gun. I felt a rush of blood down my forehead. He swung blindly again and again. I felt my right arm shatter and I dropped the can. My left hand searched desperately in the bag. I was going to fall. And when I fell. . . .

My good hand found something sharp and deadly but I

193

couldn't hang on. Reality began to recede and I was drifting . . . drifting.

I think I saw Cochran. I think I saw the scissors plunge. I think I saw him fall, silently, silently.

"Zed," I think I heard Cochran say. "Zed means zero." I think; but I wasn't sure.

It could have been another bad dream.

Forty-One

"You might have told me that reports of your death would be vastly exaggerated. I would have worried less."

My aunt was drinking a Margarita. In preparation for a long hot summer to come, she said. We were all drinking Margaritas and lounging on the terrace at The Crossing—Aunt Lydie, Bobby Blessing, Oliver Reynolds, Alexander Dana, and I. I wasn't really lounging: I had too many stitches and too much plaster for that. But I was alive, at least, and present. The fruit trees in the distance were finishing their riotous bloom. The air was seductive. We were having a preview of summer.

"She certainly looked dead when we came to get her out of the hospital in Marseille," Oliver Reynolds said crossly. "She looked as if she'd burned all her bridges and decamped." Naturally, he was furious with me. He so often was.

Aunt Lydie tried to make light of it. She had forgiven me. "Dorothy Parker once read me one of her poems before she published it. She said, 'The clouds are low along the ridges, and sweet's the air with curly smoke from all

194

my burning bridges.' I adored her, you know. Difficult, but witty.''

Blessing was perched on a delicate wicker chair that was almost as fragile and bony as he. He overwhelmed it with his sheer, improbable length. "Funny, complicated affair, this Marseille thing. But then, they usually are.''

"Tell us," Lydia Wentworth said, "all the secret things about the funny, complicated affair. You know I love secrets." She's like a child about secrets—she adores them.

"If there are secrets, you can't expect him to tell us, Lydia." Oliver was always correct about everything: he believed in playing the game, whatever it was.

But Blessing was willing, to a point. "Lassiter was British Intelligence trying to find out what had happened to a shipment of gold. The terrorist Coalition found out the gold existed and they wanted it, too. We called in Dana—terrorism is his speciality, you might say. And suddenly there we all were, wallowing in the same muddy waters. It was Persis who uncorked the bottle.''

A slightly mixed metaphor, I thought, but apt. "You mean Godzilla and me?" It was hard to talk—my broken jaw was still wired. But I could hiss enough words to be understood.

"Absolutely. You two leapt, so to speak, right into the middle of the Coalition's death squad and that really got things rolling.''

Aunt Lydie was charmed beyond measure. "Death squad? How fabulous.''

"You should know, Lydia. They almost kidnapped you.''

"Perfectly absurd of them," she said. "I never would have paid a penny.''

Blessing chose to ignore that. "You, Persis, told everything you knew to Martin. He orchestrated the whole Von Berger thing to scare you into it. That was a good thing, as it turned out, but no thanks to you. He was a greedy little bastard and the minute you spilled it all to him he

195

went right out to peddle it to the highest bidder. That turned out to be the Coalition, who promptly did him in. If they hadn't, Zed would have eventually. He knew from his sources that somebody was asking questions: he'd already done away with the two mercenaries.''

"He was so nice to that girl, Nathalie," I said regretfully.

"He was a little rat." Bobby Blessing was always the realist. He brooked no sentiment. "To be specific, he sold the information you gave him to the Coalition and they followed you from the opera house. Zed was brilliant, actually."

"Brilliant?" This was Dana for the first time. Dana obviously had no kind words for the man who had tried to kill me.

"Brilliant," Blessing mused. "He knew they were looking for him and he was more than ready. They stepped into a trap. He had it all worked out. Except for two things."

"What two things?" Oliver demanded.

"First Dana. He and his team were on the Coalition's trail. They got there minutes after the Mitzu Brigade attacked. And—" he paused for dramatic effect. We were all hanging on every word. "And except for Cochran. He never dreamed she'd kill him."

I hadn't dreamed it either. It was true . . . literally true.

"Is she all right?" Aunt Lydie asked.

"She will be. It was a bad wound—just missed a whole roster of vital organs. But she'll recover."

She'd saved my life. And because of that no one would ever know what I knew. For public consumption, she had come to the opera house just as I had, to preview the exhibition. She had been taken off just as I had by Zed's men. That was the official story and that is how it would remain. Once again, we owed each other.

"And what about Hallsey Bryce?" my aunt asked.

Blessing laughed. "His portrait will hang him eventually. To be specific, his vanity will hang him."

196

The thought of Bryce being hanged did not unduly distress Lydia Wentworth. "Serve him right," she said with conviction.

"How," Oliver wanted to know, "did you work it out about the statue, Persis?"

"I'm only guessing, but I figure that Zed probably had each of its four hollow sections cut in half again and then, with winches and sandbags and a couple of trucks, they took it down and carted it away. All they would need was about ten men working three nights. Afterward it was easy enough for Zed to get rid of the men, and that was that."

"You really gave us a scare," Dana said, "when we arrived and found you and Cochran lying there in your respective pools of blood. I'm sorry not to have arrived in time."

"You arrived in time to save us. At least we're alive."

Aunt Lydie detested the Press. "Reporters are always turning up where they're not wanted." There was a certain amount of justice in her remark. On the other hand, I too had been turning up where I was not wanted ever since this affair began, though largely by chance.

"I'm just as guilty as she."

To my surprise, Blessing disagreed. "Without you, Persis," he said grudgingly, "we might still be trying to finish it. If you hadn't told Martin, and Martin hadn't told the Coalition and Dana hadn't followed the Mitzu Brigade. . . ."

I looked at Dana. He hadn't really been listening. He was looking over our heads and beyond us at some invisible point on the horizon. He looked like a thoroughbred just before it takes the bit in its teeth.

I reached out and took his hand in my good one and squeezed it gently. There was no answering pressure.

I heard my aunt's silvery laugh. "Don't be embarrassed, Alex. She's always like this in the spring."

I looked into Dana's crystal eyes and I knew he was

197

already gone. This affair was over and he was moving on. He was not for me. Perhaps he was not for anyone.

"You are wrong, Aunt Lydie," I told her. "It has nothing to do with spring. I am just burning a bridge—a bridge I have never crossed."

For the first time I sensed summer in the air. I was free.

About the Author

Clarissa Watson is co-owner and director of The Country Art Gallery in Locust Valley, New York. She is the author of two other Peris Willum mysteries: THE FOURTH STAGE OF GAINSBOROUGH BROWN and THE BISHOP IN THE BACK SEAT, both of which are forthcoming in Ballantine editions.

The Queen of Suspense...

RUTH RENDELL